Y0-BSY-920

She must have conjured Dax into her dreams

He stood at the edge of the pool, gazing at her as she floated in a perfumed mirage. In her fantasy, when he appeared, he would look exactly as he did now, standing tall on the rocks above her, his hair swirling wildly around his face and shoulders.

Sunlight bronzed his chest and the muscles of his thighs. His eyes were dark and intense, his gaze narrowed and aflame with desire as he stared at the gentle lap of water pooling around her body.

Breath quickening, heart pounding, Carrie lifted her arms out of the water, the gesture an embrace and an invitation.

Dax jerked open the snap on his denim shorts and tore down the zipper. The cutoffs slid down his muscled thighs. He stood above her, naked.

Carrie's fantasy had just become reality.

ABOUT THE AUTHOR

For Margaret St. George, writing fills a creative
need, one she has been satisfying since she was
sixteen. She starts her stories with a single
concept, asks herself "What if...?" then begins
to formulate her characters. Using this system,
Margaret has conjured up some of the sexiest
heroes and most memorable stories in the
American Romance line. Her wit and deeply
emotional writing have made her a reader
favorite and an award winner.

Books by Margaret St. George

HARLEQUIN AMERICAN ROMANCE

HARLEQUIN INTRIGUE

Don't miss any of our special offers. Write to us at the
following address for information on our newest releases.

Harlequin Reader Service
U.S.: 3010 Walden Ave., P.O. Box 1325, Buffalo, NY 14269
Canadian: P.O. Box 609, Fort Erie, Ont. L2A 5X3

MARGARET
ST. GEORGE

THE DROP-IN BRIDE

Harlequin Books

TORONTO • NEW YORK • LONDON
AMSTERDAM • PARIS • SYDNEY • HAMBURG
STOCKHOLM • ATHENS • TOKYO • MILAN
MADRID • WARSAW • BUDAPEST • AUCKLAND

If you purchased this book without a cover you should be aware
that this book is stolen property. It was reported as "unsold and
destroyed" to the publisher, and neither the author nor the
publisher has received any payment for this "stripped book."

ISBN 0-373-16545-5

THE DROP-IN BRIDE

Copyright © 1994 by Margaret St. George.

All rights reserved. Except for use in any review, the reproduction or
utilization of this work in whole or in part in any form by any electronic,
mechanical or other means, now known or hereafter invented, including
xerography, photocopying and recording, or in any information storage
or retrieval system, is forbidden without the written permission of the
publisher, Harlequin Enterprises Limited, 225 Duncan Mill Road,
Don Mills, Ontario, Canada M3B 3K9.

All characters in this book have no existence outside the imagination of
the author and have no relation whatsoever to anyone bearing the same
name or names. They are not even distantly inspired by any individual
known or unknown to the author, and all incidents are pure invention.

This edition published by arrangement with Harlequin Enterprises B. V.

® and TM are trademarks of the publisher. Trademarks indicated with
® are registered in the United States Patent and Trademark Office, the
Canadian Trade Marks Office and in other countries.

Printed in U.S.A.

Chapter One

The first item Dax found was a red bikini top.

Actually Norman found it and brought it up from the shore. Dax suspected the parrot had been a pack rat in a past life. In a holdover from his previous incarnation, Norman scavenged the shore, trees and undergrowth and dragged any and all items he found into Dax's beach house, which the bird seemed to regard as a storage site provided for his convenience.

"So what have you got this time, Norman, old buddy?"

The scrap of bright red caught Dax's attention, and he turned away from his computer and the uninspired words faltering across the screen.

Norman tilted his head and cocked a black eye, looking pleased with himself for amusing the frustrated master of the house. He dragged his booty across the gritty floor and deposited it near a leg of the coffee table, poking and arranging the silky red material with his beak.

Dax shooed Norman aside and lifted the bikini top for inspection. A 34 C.

Transfixed, he stood in the strong tropical light spilling through the open doors, staring at the unexpected treasure while visions of bikini-clad women danced in his mind.

Finally he shook the images away and smiled at Norman. "Slow down, pal, this is only a scrap of cloth. We've been away from civilization so long that we're letting our imagination run away with us."

Even rimed with sea salt, the red material remained supple and soft to the touch, reminiscent of women themselves. For an instant Dax tried to recall when he had last stroked a woman's skin. A tactile impression of peachy velvet tingled his fingertips before he suppressed the sensation and threw Norman a mock glare.

"We chose this exile, buddy. It wasn't forced on us. And we don't want women in our lives, so stop thinking what you're thinking."

Lately he'd begun to talk to Norman as if the parrot had been a lifelong companion instead of a recent acquaintance. This from a man who, until a few weeks ago, had scoffed at people who conversed with pets.

"I know exactly the place for this prize," he decided.

What the hell. If he didn't talk to Norman, he wouldn't talk at all. And Norman was a good listener. Occasionally he fixed Dax with a beady stare as if to say, that's a crock and you know it. His flashes of superiority irritated Dax, but he conceded that Norman was usually correct in his judgments. Norman was nobody's fool. He recognized outlandish justifications when he heard them. More often he listened politely and bobbed his beak in occasional agreement, then waddled out to the deck when the conversation turned boring.

Rubbing the silky material between his thumb and forefinger, Dax followed a vine-tangled path to the storehouse located farther into the junglelike undergrowth and brought back a ladder, a nail and a hammer.

He nailed one of the thin bikini straps to the top of the flagpole at the bottom of the deck steps, then stood back to admire his handiwork, grinning as he wondered how the evening breeze would fill out the cups.

The next morning during his habitual jog along the curve of the cove, Dax noticed a neon pink bikini bottom, and a few minutes later he stumbled over a green satin pump. Both were encrusted with sea salt and half buried in the sand. An hour later, Norman brought him a lace-trimmed green garter belt.

After that, it was impossible to work. Dax spent the morning speculating about the items and the woman who had lost them. He hadn't found any debris from a shipwreck, so he concluded that some woman must have thrown the clothing overboard. Concocting various scenarios diverted him for several hours.

The next morning, near the high-water mark, he discovered a green cocktail dress—size eight—a bit faded by sun and salt water, but otherwise salvageable. When he found a tube of coral lipstick, he abandoned his jog and searched the shoreline.

A bicycle wheel and a broken piece of what looked like a child's sand bucket turned up, but no other women's items. Nothing out of the ordinary ever washed up on his beach. The recent trove he attributed to the storm of two days past. The sea was still running high, swirling with silt and sand, tossing seaweed and kelp onto the shore in larger than usual amounts.

The lipstick, he discovered, had melted in the heat of the tropical sun, and he had a devil of a time getting the smears off his hands. Since he didn't know what to do with the green dress, he spread it over the deck rail to dry, then hung it in his closet. The sight provided a mild shock. It had been a long time since his clothing had shared space with anything feminine.

Which, he reminded himself and Norman, was exactly how he wanted it. There would be no more women in Dax Stone's life, no more serious relationships, no more disappointments or failed expectations. There would be no wife in his future, no family. It hadn't been easy, but Dax believed he had finally come to terms with a solitary future. Staring at the green dress, he wondered if he really had.

Even without a relationship, his future was not bleak by any means. He had good friends, the freedom to do as he liked and go where he liked, no money worries, and he was fortunate enough to enjoy a satisfying and successful career.

Except...

Frowning and ignoring the quiet hum of his computer, he carried a tall glass of iced tea to the deck and leaned on the railing. Overhead the sky was clear and blazing with tropical heat, the air heavy with humidity. A riot of scents assailed his nostrils, the chaotic mingling of various perfumes wafting from several dozen species of tropical blossoms.

His career... Thinking about it drew his brows into an unconscious frown.

Chewing on a chunk of ice, he watched the waves crash against an outcropping of rocks that jutted into the sea, forming one arm of the cove.

"We're in trouble, Norm, old buddy." Staring at the sea, he fought a silent battle against the frustration tightening his chest. He refused to call it panic. "We can't produce anymore. The words come but they have no life. They don't mean anything."

Norman didn't care. He'd heard this complaint before. Norman was more interested in quarreling with his friends who hopped from tree limb to tree limb arguing about important parrot matters.

Dax tossed Norman the slice of lemon from his tea and considered inspecting the shore for more of the woman's wardrobe.

Anything to avoid facing his computer.

Norman cocked his head and gave Dax a look so humanly disdainful that Dax laughed aloud.

"Okay, okay, work it is. Slave driver."

Turning away from the siren call of the beach, Dax walked on bare feet into his house. He used that term loosely. His house—he thought of it as the torture chamber—consisted of one large, bright room hemmed by a deck that extended around all four sides.

Delaying, he rinsed his glass in the sink, glancing across the room at his unmade bed and thinking he should wash the sheets and the clothing in the growing pile on the closet floor. In fact, it wouldn't hurt to do a little housecleaning. The place was littered with leaves and small twigs, an accumulation of sand and shells that he and Norman had tracked inside. The cushions on a scattered collection of wicker furniture were buried beneath stacks of books and papers. If he didn't run the dishwasher today, he would be out of clean plates and cups tomorrow.

No, he told himself firmly. He would write today. He'd consider doing housework tomorrow. Or the next day.

Examining the mess he was living in, it occurred to Dax that man swiftly reverted to a slovenly nature if left to his own devices. It wasn't a flattering thought, but he could live with it. Excessive neatness was not one of his vices.

Living on an isolated island gave one the freedom to fully concentrate on the things that mattered, the world of ideas and concepts, without the distraction of dealing with artificially imposed standards. Such as housecleaning. Or shaving, he thought, stroking a hand down a fast-growing beard that was approaching hermit length.

Every day he checked the beard's progress in a hand mirror, enjoying a rebel's delight in the wild, slightly dangerous aspect the beard gave to his face. This must have been how Robinson Crusoe looked. Hair approaching shoulder length, a dark mustache flowing into a full-bodied facial brush. It was every man's secret desire to discover how he would look in a full-face beard. A beard was a statement of manhood.

And Dax was feeling a little shaky on the question of his manhood. With good reason. A scowl tightened his expression. *Forget it,* he warned himself. *There's nothing you can do.*

He watched Norman drag the lemon peel through the doorway, then glanced toward the closet. For the past two days, Jane Doe, whoever she was, had flitted in and out of his thoughts attired in a red or neon pink bikini or a filmy green dress. Size eight, thirty-four C. She wore coral lipstick and cared enough about details to dye her pumps to match her dress and choose a matching garter belt.

By now he knew all about her. She was tall and red-haired. Her breasts were full and seductively rounded. She had shapely legs that climbed forever. She was in her late twenties, old enough to have experienced a generous taste of life, but not old enough to be jaded. She owned the world's largest bookstore and sold the hell out of Dax's books. In her spare time she modeled swimwear, starred in art films and advised President Clinton. She loved sex, seductive lingerie, great books, football and fast cars. Marriage was the furthest thing from her mind. She did not want children.

Dax stared at Norman. "Forget it, pal. Women like that don't exist. Besides, you're through with women. Remember? And they're through with you," he added bitterly.

He rubbed his face, combing the bristly growth with his fingertips, suddenly wishing he had someone present to tell him if the beard suited him or if he was just hiding behind a face full of fuzz. But there was no one on the island but himself. And he had no idea where the thought came from that he might have grown the beard to hide from himself. He dismissed that ridiculous notion at once.

The point of the island was to escape all distractions. No people, no interruptions. Just him and the computer.

And the book that wouldn't be born.

Leaning on the kitchen counter, avoiding a sticky spot, Dax glared at the blank computer screen, hating it.

Eventually, he made himself lift a stack of pages from the end of the counter. He skimmed a couple of paragraphs and released a sigh of frustration. Skillfully written crap, that's all it was.

It was time to have another page burning on the beach and consign his do-nothing characters with all their profound and boring dialogue to ashes. Time to knock the chapters out of his computer and start over. Yet again.

He ordered himself to clear his mind and stop thinking about vampires and werewolves, his usual fictional subjects.

He had come here with a good plot, damn it. His agent thought so, too. So what had happened to that great plot? Why wasn't it coming together?

Maybe a cup of coffee. Caffeine would get the juices flowing.

Damn it, he didn't understand what was happening to him. Never before had he suffered a dry spell. He was famed for his prolific production.

And he produced in the midst of noisy chaos and multiple interruptions. Hiring a secretary hadn't eased the burden. There were calls he simply had to take, decisions only he could make. His secretary earned her salary by dealing with the weekly sacks of mail from his readers. But still he felt an obligation to at least scan the letters. His readers weren't writing to his secretary, they were writing to Dax Stone.

Then there were radio, television and print interviews. His publisher and Mort Lewan, his agent, pushed him to promote his books even though his name was world famous. More often than he liked, he caved in and allowed himself to be trotted out on the early morning talk show circuit.

And then there was the reading. Every novelist working in horror and fantasy wanted a quote from Dax Stone. They wanted, in fact, to *be* the next Dax Stone.

Remembering how it had been made his stomach knot. He had felt as if tiny invisible hands plucked at his skin, tearing off little bits of flesh, slowly reducing him to walking bones.

At that point he had been sleeping three hours a night, worrying incessantly, trying to write in brief snatches of borrowed time.

It was his agent, a man who possessed the sensitivity of a crocodile, who finally spotted the obvious.

"The new book is okay," Mort had said over lunch at Regine's, dragging out the words.

"But?"

"But it reminds me too much of *Dark Blood*. It's not the same novel, but it's close enough that I kept thinking I'd read it before."

Until that moment Dax had only suspected that he'd cannibalized himself. No wonder the book had flowed so well, had seemed almost effortless. He had written it before.

"When a writer starts rewriting his early books... Well, certain people—and you know which reviewers I'm talking about—might say that's a sign of burnout." Morton had leaned back in his chair and studied Dax through the smoke curling from the tip of an imported cigar. "You don't look too good. Are you sleeping all right? Remembering to eat? I'm worried about you."

That's all it had taken for the frustrations to pour forth. When the explosion ended, Dax ran his hand down the length of a two-hundred-dollar tie, then pressed his fingers to the line between his eyes.

"Damn it, Mort. I don't have time to write anymore. I don't know if I *want* to write anymore, at least not horror. Maybe I've said all I have to say in this area."

"Horror is what made you rich and famous."

"Point taken. But maybe it's time to move on." Leaning back in his chair, he frowned across the restaurant, drumming his fingertips against the tabletop. "Maybe it's time to write the book I've always wanted to write, the *big* book."

"What kind of big book?" Morton asked cautiously.

Dax spun out just enough of his idea to start the dollar signs rolling behind Mort's eyes.

"The reviewers couldn't ignore this one." Excitement flushed Mort's cheeks, "They'd have to take you seriously." He knew it irked the hell out of Dax that reviewers dismissed him as merely a genre writer. All his books had topped the *New York Times* bestseller list and stayed there for months. But the reviewers still treated his work like a print version of a low-budget movie.

"Right now all I've got is a bare-bones concept. But I know there's a book here. A hell of a book."

"So what's it going to take?"

"I need a year. No interruptions, no distractions. I need to get away from ringing phones and outside demands, away from everyone and everything."

Thus began the great experiment.

A week later Morton had phoned with an interesting proposition. One of his clients had an ex-husband who wanted to sell an island in the Caribbean. It was inaccessible and isolated. It sounded like Dax's idea of heaven.

"That type of utter solitude would drive anyone else crazy," Mort said, "but it might be just what you're looking for."

Dax bought the island sight unseen. While he worked out previous commitments, he had a house built, furnished, and a generator installed. He and Mort planned the details of his great escape.

Three months ago, and without a backward glance, Dax had walked away from the chaos that was his life. As far as the world was concerned, Dax Stone vanished. Only Mort knew where he was, and Mort wasn't talking. Mort knew the publicity value of keeping his mouth closed and letting the mystery build.

Dax gazed at the tropical growth exploding around him, and listened to the sounds of nature. The solitude was exactly what he had needed. He hadn't suffered a minute's regret.

Everything he wanted and needed was here on the island. Plus the luxury of quiet and unscheduled time. He hadn't enjoyed this much privacy since his first book.

He had nine months left to luxuriate in doing nothing but writing his big novel.

There was only one problem.

He, who had never suffered a single second of writer's block, was suddenly unable to produce compelling prose. His work had become about as fascinating as the side panel on a cereal box.

Some days he couldn't write at all. It was a new and frightening experience. Gut-wrenching.

Cursing, Dax aimed his coffee cup at the nearest coconut palm and threw the mug hard enough that it broke in two pieces against the trunk and shattered into the underbrush below.

He didn't know what the hell was the matter with him.

He'd developed a strange hollow feeling behind his rib cage that was starting to concern him. He didn't feel pressured, and it wasn't stress. It wasn't hunger or thirst. It couldn't be loneliness, as he had a solitary nature and had decided years ago that he didn't need people in his life. He didn't feel ill. So why did the hollow spot seem to be growing?

What was missing from his life?

Ten lousy pages and a Spam sandwich later, Dax stood on the deck, watching the sun sink toward a watery horizon. Streaks of pink and orange smudged the sky. If he was going to search for more of Jane Doe's discarded clothing, now was the time to do it, before full darkness descended.

After draining the last drops of a cold beer and tossing Norman and his girlfriend the leftover Spam, he gathered an armload of manuscript pages and a butane lighter.

Following a path between tall rustling palms and blooming oleander shrubs, he walked to the beach and located the fire pit he'd dug three drafts ago. Burning his work was becoming a tradition. He would start the fire with eight wadded pages, then sit staring into the blaze as he fed the chapters into the flames.

He spotted the rubber boat the instant he stepped onto the powdered coral beach. A gift from the sea. At once his spirits rose. How had it gone adrift and found his island? Was it Jane Doe's boat?

After placing the manuscript pages in the fire pit and anchoring them against the breeze with a rock, he headed for the boat, striding past feathery piles of seaweed and the sand crabs exploring the fronds.

The rubber boat was indeed a prize, the largest item so far to wash up on his shore.

He approached near enough to notice dried salt powdering the dark, rounded rim. The name *Lady Marge* was stenciled on the side, perhaps the name of the ship or yacht it had come from. Lost overboard during the recent storm? It seemed likely.

If there were oars inside, Dax decided he would keep the boat and use it for fishing in the cove.

A moan startled him, so unexpected that he frowned and turned on his bare heel, scanning the dense tropical growth at the top of the beach.

But the moan came from the boat.

Curious, he walked closer and peered inside.

A woman lay sprawled on the bottom of the boat, and she was in bad shape. Her swollen face and arms were sunburned to a red crisp. Her lips were cracked and oozing clear fluid. There was a gash above one eye, and a deep scratch near the cuff of her shorts.

First the sea had brought him a woman's clothing. Now the waves had yielded the woman herself. At least he assumed this was the woman who owned the clothing he had found.

Stepping into the boat, Dax knelt and brushed back a tangle of wet dark hair, then pressed his fingers behind her ear. He found a pulse, but it was weak and thready.

This was not a lucky woman. She needed serious medical attention and care. Instead, she had washed up on his beach. He didn't know squat about first aid.

The only thing he did know was he had to get her inside. Pushing his hands carefully beneath her, he lifted her in his arms.

Before he could decide what to do with her, her eyelids fluttered, then flickered open. Dax looked into green, green eyes, the loveliest dark-fringed eyes he had ever seen. Visions of green glass sparkled in his mind. Sunlight pouring through the Mediterranean. The green, green grass of home.

She stared into his face, then before Dax could utter a reassurance, rasped a croaking scream of panic or fear. Her body stiffened and then fell limp in his arms.

Chapter Two

In the dream Carrie was roasting in hell, tied to a large spit that rotated over roaring flames. She was being cooked, and the pain was intense. When the spit turned full circle, she could see Michael. It gave her grim pleasure to know he was in hell, too, but it infuriated her that he looked a whole lot cooler and more comfortable than she was.

Groaning, Carrie turned on her side, and the dream shifted to a broiling courtroom. Michael was chatting with a bevy of starlets and models surrounding his lawyer's table, ignoring Carrie, who sat in a flaming witness chair. A sad-eyed woman, dressed in a judge's robe, pointed an accusing finger at her. Arrows of fire shot from the woman's fingertip and charred Carrie's stomach.

A large hand cupped her head and lifted her, shattering the nightmares. Cool water trickled over her lips. When she felt the lip of a glass against her teeth, she drank eagerly, gulping the liquid as fast as she could swallow. The hand lowered her head to a pillow, and instantly she spiraled back into burning dreams.

Dax knelt beside the bed, watching her with an anxious expression. Her face and eyelids were less swollen than they had been, but her legs, arms and chest were fiery red and blistered. She burned with fever and had been delirious for two days, drifting in and out of consciousness.

Carefully he drew back the sheet covering her naked body. He'd removed her clothing because her shorts and tank top were salt-stiff and soiled.

"Let me have your arm," he said in a low voice even though he knew she didn't hear him. After squeezing a lump of cool burn ointment into his palm, he smoothed it across the back of her burned hand and slowly worked up her arm to the elbow, then to her shoulder. The tank top had exposed her stomach so she was burned there, too. He treated her waist and upper hips, listening as she moaned and whimpered.

After he treated the front of her, he gently turned her on her stomach and spread ointment over the backs of her legs, working up toward her thighs, then he coated the burned area between her upper back and her buttocks.

As Dax massaged the ointment over her skin, he tried to recall if there was anything else he could do to help her. Every half hour he made her drink something. Getting liquids into her was vital, he knew. Into the bouillon, clear soup and juice he dissolved aspirin to combat her fever.

After covering her with a light sheet, Dax cleaned the ointment off his hands, then sat facing her. Pain and distress flickered across her face. Every now and then she mumbled, sometimes she murmured a name that might have been Michael.

Curiosity consumed him. Who was she? What was she doing alone in a rubber boat on the vast ocean? Were people searching for her?

And what was he going to do with her?

"What do you think, Norman? Is she going to make it?"

Norman had been busy lately. He'd brought home a pair of ivory-colored women's panties, a shiny button, several seedpods and a silver hoop earring. The button entranced him to the point that he ignored Dax entirely.

"I think so, too. She's going to make it." He sipped a beer, watching the rise and fall of her breasts beneath the light sheet.

Oddly, he didn't find her nakedness arousing. He noticed her body, of course, but his anxiety regarding her survival was so acute that he saw her primarily as a patient thrust into his reluctant care.

He couldn't pinpoint when that attitude changed, but by the eighth day, when he was certain that she would fully recover, Dax realized he had developed a high degree of discomfort when he treated her with the ointment. Mouth dry, he studiously avoided looking at her breasts or the tops of her thighs. He battled not to notice the smooth softness of her skin or the delicate structure of her wrists and collarbone.

But as the swelling diminished and she began to heal, he became increasingly aware of her as a woman—a woman with a stunningly beautiful and desirable body. She was small but perfectly proportioned, lush breasts giving way to a curve of waist and flare of hips. He found himself battling thoughts that were anything but disinterested.

His reaction embarrassed and irritated him. The irritation sprang from the realization that he was not responding well to the first test of his vow never to involve himself with another woman.

In his defense, the possibility hadn't occurred to him that a beautiful, naked stranger might turn up in his bed. Such an unexpected circumstance would test any man.

Disturbed, he jerked out his chair and sat down in front of his computer. Maybe a few hours of work would shift his thoughts away from soft curves and throaty murmurs. He didn't think so, but it was worth a try.

GRADUALLY CARRIE BECAME aware that she was healing, getting stronger by the minute. It seemed that she was awake for longer periods, but it was difficult to tell if the periods of wakefulness were daydream or reality.

Once her eyelids blinked open and she imagined she was in a huge room, maybe a library. Wherever she looked she saw books and piles of paper. A Neanderthal man, naked as near as she could tell, sat in front of a computer terminal, tapping at the keys.

His long, dark hair brushed wide, muscled shoulders that moved beneath smooth, deeply tanned skin, oddly arousing to watch. A deep valley defined his spine. His torso narrowed from shoulders to waist in classic male form. Seen from behind, he was, in fact, a perfect and fascinating male specimen.

Beneath his typing chair, Carrie saw the backs of heavy calves. At first she thought he was wearing pinkish-white socks, then realized he must have been walking on the beach and his feet were still covered by fine powdered coral.

As she watched, puzzled by this strange dream, the Neanderthal shoved back from the computer, stared at the monitor a minute, then brought his fists down on the desktop. Before Carrie drifted again into a hot restless sleep, she thought he shouted, "Crap!"

Eventually she understood that the librarylike room was real and she was lying on a bed on one side of it. The Neanderthal was real, too. Because she didn't know who he was or where she was, she pretended to sleep more than she actually did, studying him through her lashes and trying to remember what had happened to her. The last scene with Michael returned in bits and pieces, not all of it making sense.

There was a secret, she knew that much. Something wonderful and terrible all wrapped in one. But she couldn't remember the secret. Her mind pulled back when she edged close to remembering. To ease the panic she experienced on those occasions, she focused her full attention on the man.

If Carrie ignored his hairy face, she had to concede that he was an erotically handsome man. Sun-bronzed skin stretched taut over a tall, big-boned body that was muscular enough to suggest he worked out regularly. Judging by his heavy calves and thighs, she guessed he probably ran or jogged. Maybe he belonged to a health club.

Whatever form of exercise he preferred, it was working for him. He was big but lean and taut. He had a gorgeous body, and Carrie was able to see most of it because the only thing he ever wore was a pair of cutoff jeans that hung low on his hips and ended just below well-shaped buttocks.

But the beard repelled her. Because of it, she couldn't make out his features, only his eyes. At night his eyes seemed very dark, but in the daylight and when he bent near her, they seemed hazel, a warm combination of soft brown and gold.

Occasionally he went outside and left her alone for an hour or so, but usually he worked at the computer or lay in his hammock, reading. He talked to himself a lot. As far as Carrie could tell, he had no friends and not much contact with the world outside this room. No one came to visit. The telephone never rang. If the mailman ever arrived at the door, she had missed it.

What Carrie didn't understand, and what made her uneasy, was why he hadn't notified the authorities immediately after finding her. Why had he kept her here instead of taking her to the nearest hospital?

It frightened her to think that maybe he was as crazy as he sometimes acted.

Clearly she had to get out of here as soon as she could. She couldn't recall the exact details, but a pressure in her chest told her there were urgent reasons she had to get home. Something to do with the secret that she couldn't quite remember.

One thing at a time, she told herself, drawing a calming breath. First she had to get on her feet and away from wherever she was.

"How long are you going to keep pretending that you're still sick and half-conscious?"

The Neanderthal's deep baritone startled her and made her twitch. Cautiously, Carrie opened one eye and discovered he was sprawled in one of the wicker chairs, bare legs thrust out before him, fingers tented beneath the edge of his beard, staring at her. "I know you're awake and that you can hear me."

"I . . . I beg your . . . pardon?" she asked. Her voice sounded raspy and unused. Opening both eyes, she regarded him warily.

"It's time to quit playing possom. You and I need to talk." The beard made it impossible to gauge his expression.

"I'm feeling a lot better," Carrie admitted. She knew she had been very ill. But she also knew she had been well for a couple of days.

"I'm no doctor, but I think you've been conscious for at least three days." His stare made him look absolutely menacing. "So why are you pretending that you're still out of it?"

"Did you say *three days?*" Shock brought her to a sitting position, which was when she discovered she was naked. It hadn't been a dream. Blushing furiously, she grabbed the sheet and yanked it up to cover her breasts. "How long have I been here?"

Dark eyes flicked to the sheet curving over her breasts. "Ten days."

Carrie's eyes widened until they ached. "Ten . . . That can't be true!" After a minute, she swung her legs over the side of the bed, fought a wave of dizziness, then wrapped the sheet more firmly around her body. She didn't like the way the Neanderthal was looking at her chest, like she was a bonbon and he was a sugar addict. But . . . ten days. She had to get to a telephone, and fast.

"Listen, I have to make some calls right now. A couple are long distance. I'll pay you for them." Feeling a fizz of panic, she turned her head, searching the clutter for a phone cord.

Ten days. And she must have been drifting in the boat for at least two or three days. That meant she was in real trouble with her editor.

Terry had agreed to hold her job for five days, not a minute longer. She was way past the deadline he'd set. The only thing that might make him reconsider was if she returned with a big, *big* story. But she'd better walk into the press room dragging Elvis behind her or she could kiss off her job. It was gone.

"I don't have a telephone."

Disbelief clouded her eyes. "Come on, everyone has a telephone!"

Before she could deal with Terry, she had to deal with this man. And she'd better watch her step, Carrie thought suddenly, studying him. He could be a recluse, that was possible, or he could just be flaming crazy. All things considered, it occurred to her that everything pointed toward this guy being a weirdo. And that was frightening.

She tugged the sheet higher over her breasts, growing more uncomfortable by the minute. Where were her clothes? And how much of the rubbing along her naked body was dream and how much had been reality? Exactly how big a problem did she have here?

"I'm sorry," he said. Actually, he didn't sound as menacing as he looked. "But the nearest telephone is about twenty-five miles that way. On the next island." He jerked a thumb over his bare shoulder.

Nobody, but nobody lived in today's world without a phone. Either he was lying or he didn't want her to tell anyone where she was. The implication lurking in the latter possibility was enough to raise goose bumps on Carrie's warm skin.

"Ah...who are you?" she asked, rubbing at the bumps on her arms. "I'd like to know who to thank for rescuing me." She tried for a smile, but her lips thinned into something more like anxiety. The place was such a cluttered pit that her top and shorts could be under her nose, buried beneath all the papers and books, and she'd never see them.

"The question is...who are *you*?"

So that's how it was going to be. All right, she didn't have much choice. She'd play it his way if that would get her into her clothes and out of here. The sooner, the better. She'd phone her editor from one of the telephones at the airport.

"My name is Caroline James. Carrie. I'm a reporter for the *Denver Post*." That should give him pause. Even an ax murderer should have better sense than to hack up a newspaper reporter. The front page would fry his butt. Her editor would demand the electric chair.

And if by chance her rescuer-captor was not an ax murderer, well, then, the fact that she was a reporter could still work to her advantage. Everyone wanted to be interviewed, to see his name in the newspaper. She would ask him a few questions, pander to his ego a bit, then wave bye-bye and scoot right out of here.

He stiffened. Every hair on his head, face, chest and legs seemed to bristle. Jumping from his chair, he paced across the dirty floor, flinging out his arms.

"You people are absolutely shameless! Mort warned me that something like this could happen. He told me everyone would look for me, that one of you vultures might actually show up on my doorstep. I didn't believe him."

"Excuse me?" Carrie stared at him in astonishment.

"I could have sworn that I covered my tracks." He shoved a hand through flying dark hair. "I traveled under a different name, I doubled back, I paid Dingy Bill a small fortune to bring me out here with the understanding that he wouldn't tell a soul about it!" He stared at her. "You people really have nerve, I'll give you that. You'll do anything for a story, won't you? Even risk getting yourself killed."

"I knew it," she whispered. "You're a murderer."

"I'm talking about you damned near dying from dehydration and sunstroke!" He flung a hand toward the door and the shore beyond. "You were half dead when I found you. Can you possibly believe this story is worth it? What if you'd washed up on the other side of the island? Have you thought about that? I wouldn't have found you, and you'd be dead now!"

"Excuse me, but exactly what story are we talking about?"

She didn't have the details, but Carrie thought she was starting to get the picture. He was on the run, she decided, a criminal of some type. He hadn't notified anyone about finding her because he feared being recognized and apprehended.

Suddenly she realized the obvious. The worst thing she could have done was identify herself as a reporter. Naturally he would believe that she had sought him out for the purpose of revealing his whereabouts. Intrepid girl reporter succeeds where police fail. Not bad, actually. But a little scary.

"The truth is," she admitted slowly, doing some backpedaling, "I used to be a reporter, but not anymore. My editor, a real snake, fired me."

He gave her a look of disgust as he paced past her. "I pity the fool who believes anything you people say! First you're a reporter, now suddenly you're not. You'll say whatever you think I want to hear, right?"

Carrie contemplated the cut healing on her leg, her mind racing. An agitated criminal was a dangerous criminal. First priority—tell him anything, but calm him down.

"Okay. I'll admit I was a reporter when I flew to the Caribbean. But all I want to do is tell your side of the story." She hoped to heaven that she was playing this right.

She racked her brain, trying to recall recent crimes and who he might be. If she was lucky this would be the big story she needed for Terry, and she would live to write it and turn it in.

"My side of the story?" He stopped pacing and stared at her, sweeping a look over the sheet clutched to her breasts and her long legs sticking out beneath. "What on earth are you talking about?"

There was something almost familiar about him, Carrie decided, but she couldn't pull the information to the front of her brain. But watching him move, listening to his voice, Carrie experienced a growing impression that she should know who he was.

So where could she have seen him? On a wanted poster at the post office? On the nightly news? Front page of a newspaper? No, the voice was sort of familiar, too. Had she met him before? It didn't seem likely.

She would have remembered a guy with a fabulous body and a D.J.'s seductive baritone.

Still, she had an odd feeling she sort of knew him, might even have been attracted to him at one time. That thought was so strange she almost rolled her eyes and smiled.

He stalked over to the bed, planted his fists on his hips and glared at her. Carrie asked herself how Lois Lane would have handled an intimidating glare, then lifted her chin and met his dark eyes. The point was not to let him see that he made her nervous.

"I'm beginning to think I was wrong. You didn't come here intentionally looking for me."

He stood directly in front of her. When she dropped her glance, she discovered she was at eye level to his low-slung, cutoff jeans. Carrie wet her lips and looked away from the arrow of dark hair sliding down gorgeous ripples of washboard muscle and disappearing behind a snap and zipper.

"Maybe I did and maybe I didn't," she said, trying frantically to guess what he wanted her to say.

"All right, tell me my name."

"Ah . . . Rumpelstiltskin?" she offered with a weak smile, trying not to stare at his heavy, well-shaped thighs. That perfect male body was distracting her from the crucial question. What were his intentions? "Look, you aren't going to hurt me, are you? This was all just a mistake. You're right, I wasn't looking for you. I just . . ."

"Hurt you?" His eyebrows soared in an expression of incredulity. "I *saved* you!" A minute passed. A very long minute, while he studied her pale face and fidgeting hands. "You don't have a clue who I am," he said finally, speaking softly.

"Well . . . no."

"Great!" The hair around his lower face shifted upward in what Carrie hopefully interpreted as a smile. "Now, let's try again. How did you turn up on my beach?"

Since she didn't seem to have any bargaining power, Carrie decided she might as well tell him. "It's a depressing story." Lifting a hand, she rubbed her forehead and discovered a scab over her right eye. "I told Terry—that's my snake editor—I was looking for that missing writer, what's his name, and the trail led toward the Caribbean. Actually that was just a cover. I flew straight to San Salvador to meet Michael Medlin, a guy I once thought I might be in love with."

She stared at the gritty floor, feeling a stab of panic behind her rib cage. "Something came up . . ." Why couldn't she remember what the something was? "And it was imperative that I talk to Michael immediately." She paused, frowning with the effort to remember. "We talked, all right. And guess what? The lying bastard is married."

"This is a riveting tale, Miss James, but exactly what does it have to do with you washing up on my beach?"

"I'm getting to that part," she said testily. She drew a long breath and tightened the sheet across her breasts. For an instant, she'd thought the secret was about to return to her. Now it was gone again.

"I met Michael on his yacht, the *Lady Marge*. Wouldn't you know, his wife's name is Marge. Anyway, we were two days at sea before we had the big, and I mean *big* fight. I stomped up on deck, threw my overnight bag in a rubber boat and climbed inside the boat to sit a while and cool off. I was upset and mad as hell." Except she couldn't recall what they had fought about. Probably about Michael being married. But there was something more.

"It was storming, right?"

Carrie nodded. "To make a long story short, something bad happened. Maybe the yacht capsized. Maybe it just tilted hard to the right. I don't know. Anyway, I ended up in the water. Me and the boat. I screamed, but I guess Michael and his friends didn't hear. When the sun rose, there was no sign of the yacht. I was alone on the sea without food, water or shade. I don't know how long I was out there before I washed up here. Wherever here is. Anyway, that's what happened." Her shoulders lifted in a sigh. "I told you it was a depressing story."

He sat down in a wicker chair, studying her with those intent brown-and-gold eyes. "Is anyone else looking for the missing writer?"

Carrie lifted her head and blinked. "I don't believe you! I open my heart, I tell you about Michael and about him being married, about me set adrift and almost dying, and the only part that interests you is the story I told my editor so I could get out of Denver?"

Then she had it. The pieces dropped, click, click, click, into place. Hiding from the public, resenting reporters, the stacks of what she now realized were manuscript pages, the computer.

Her mouth dropped. "You're Dax Stone! You're the writer who vanished!"

He covered his eyes with a hand. "There are two billion people in the world and it has to be a reporter who washes up on my beach."

Excitement flared in Carrie's green eyes. She almost let go of the sheet she clutched to her chest. "Listen, do you know that every reporter in the English-speaking world is looking for you? Of course you know." Her mind sped a mile a minute.

She had an opportunity to scoop *People, USA Today, Time* and *Newsweek*. Terry would not only let her keep her job, he would roll out a red carpet and spread it with roses. Dax Stone was no Elvis, but right now he was the next best thing. And she was sitting smack in the middle of his hideaway, staring at the pages of his next blockbuster.

This was the story of a career. There might be movie possibilities if she dramatized the rescue a bit. Excitement heated her brain. She couldn't wait to get to a typewriter and a telephone.

"I've seen you on *Good Morning, America*," she said, looking around for her clothes. "It was the beard that put me off." Now that she knew he wasn't an ax murderer she could be brave. "You should lose the beard, by the way. It doesn't do a thing for you. Where are my clothes? This has been interesting, and I'm grateful that you rescued me, but I have to go now." A radiant smile lit her face. "Do you have any idea how exciting this is?"

"Your clothes are over there," he said, pointing to a pile of fabric creeping out of his closet. "You're going to go straight to a phone and inform your newspaper where I am, is that your intention?"

"You bet it is," Carrie said happily. "I might even win a prize for this story. *The Enquirer* thinks you're dead, did you know that? One of the other tabloids insists you were abducted by aliens. They have witnesses who will swear to it."

Standing, she wrapped the sheet tightly around her body and wobbled toward the closet. She wasn't feeling one hundred percent yet, but the adrenaline was flowing so high she didn't really notice.

Dax watched her bend to sort out her clothes from his. "You don't care why I wanted—no, needed—some time alone? It doesn't bother you even a little that I don't want to be found?"

"Geez," she said, making a face and holding up her shorts. The cut on her leg had bled all over them. She almost asked why he hadn't washed them, then stopped herself. People as rich and famous as Dax Stone didn't do laundry.

"Are you listening to anything I'm saying?"

"You're news and I'm a reporter," she called over her shoulder, digging through his cutoffs and dirty underwear. She found her tank top and held it up in triumph even though blood spots dotted the front. It was wrinkled and sun-faded. "I'm really sorry if revealing your whereabouts is going to be an inconvenience, but I don't have a choice."

"Of course you do. What if I asked you—as a favor to the person who saved your life—not to tell anyone where I am?"

"I hope you won't do that because I'd feel really bad. But I'd still have to write the story." She found her bra and panties, and finally her sandals. "Stop staring at me like that," she said uncomfortably. "You have to know this isn't personal.'' The accusation in his brown eyes made her turn to one side. "Look, I need this exclusive. It'll save my job."

"A salamander has a higher moral sense than a reporter does. Women reporters are the worst."

Stung, Carrie spread her hands, then grabbed at the descending sheet. "I'm only doing my job. I have rent to pay. I have to feed myself and keep Visa off my back. I have a cat and two goldfish who depend on me." She kicked through the pile of clothing on the floor and stepped into the closet to dress, shouting through the door. "If it wasn't me, it would be someone else. You must know that."

"One last time—I'm asking you to respect my privacy."

She emerged from the stifling closet, tugging down the tank top. "You're only making this harder for both of us." She looked around the large untidy room, imprinting details on her mind so she could describe them. "I don't suppose you'd tell me what you're working on," she suggested, trying to get a peek at the words on the computer screen. He scowled at her, his expression furious. She dropped her eyes and blushed. "You're right. That was out of line."

"I opened my house to you. I fed you and nursed you. I treated your cuts and the worst case of sunburn I've ever seen."

"And I'm grateful! Honest. You probably saved my life!" Guilt was not a good quality in a reporter. Like Terry said, you told the story and moved on. But sometimes that was difficult advice to follow.

Dax Stone's glare suggested that she had overstayed her welcome. He sat sprawled in the wicker chair, staring at her like she was a loathsome bug.

She edged toward the door. After patting the pockets of her shorts, she stopped and gave him a look of dismay. "It seems that I've misplaced my wallet."

"What a shame."

A rush of color flooded her face. "So, ah, would you mind lending me twenty dollars?"

He made a sound of disgust. "You're really something, you know that? Well, you're out of luck. I don't keep any cash in the house."

Carrie's shoulders lifted in a sigh. If she believed Dax Stone didn't have a phone and didn't have any ready cash, then her IQ had sunk lower than her bra size.

"Okay, I understand why you don't want to make this easy for me." She dusted her hands across the front of her wrinkled and bloody shorts.

"No offense, but your hair looks like hell. And those clothes... Are you sure you want to go out in public looking like that?"

Carrie stiffened her shoulders. "Cheap shot, Stone. There's no reason for you to be so damned nasty. It's not my fault that you're a celebrity or that you decided to disappear. Look, you have to understand—you're big news. And *I* found you."

"You found me," he repeated, his eyes as hard as brown rocks. "The way I recall it, *I'm* the one who found *you.*"

"You know what I mean." She could feel her cheeks flaming. "No offense, but you're a lot more personable and charming on the talk shows than you are in person."

So, okay, she could see why he might not want to let her use his phone. But to send her out penniless seemed petty and small. Now she would have to work up her courage and beg a quarter from a stranger.

She thrust out her hand and tried to smile. "Look, thanks for everything. I deeply appreciate all you did to help me."

Although his handshake was impersonal, his hand was big and warm and familiar enough to shoot a tingle down Carrie's spine. Frowning, she remembered those arousing hands gently smoothing cooling lotion over her naked body.

This man had undressed her and had seen her naked. He had run his hands over her breast and hips and listened to her groans of pleasure. Swallowing hard, she snatched her hand back and rubbed her palm against the side of her shorts.

Turning toward the door, she quickly walked away from him. "Well, thanks again. Which direction is the street?"

"There isn't one."

"Nice try," she said, smiling, feeling strangely reluctant to leave. It seemed wrong somehow to jump up and leave after ten days, and she felt bad that they were parting on unpleasant terms.

Carrie would have liked to know Dax better now that she'd learned who he was. However, she could discover everything she needed for her article by browsing through back issues of any newsmagazine. And, too, the longer she delayed phoning in his whereabouts, the better chance that someone would scoop her. "Never mind. It can't be too hard to find a street." She gave him a look over her shoulder. "Bye. I wish we'd met under different circumstances."

He glared at her. "Responsible adults don't repay hospitality by stabbing their host in the back."

Carrie ground her teeth together and wiggled her fingers in a wave. There were parts of her job that she absolutely hated.

Dax leaned against the doorjamb and watched her hurry down the steps, noticing that she gripped the railing and appeared a little wobbly on her feet. He was frankly amazed by her energy. He wasn't sure he could have spent ten days in bed, then jumped up and dashed off. Of course she'd been faking for a couple of those days. Why? He didn't have any idea. Possibly she was studying him to gather material for the exposé she planned to write.

At the bottom of the steps, she paused and examined the bikini top fluttering atop the pole, then she drew a deep breath and headed toward the beach.

This, he decided, was definitely a cold-beer occasion. He took a beer from his small fridge, popped the tab and carried it out to the deck chair facing the cove.

Thirty minutes later he saw her puffing up the path to the house. She narrowed her eyes at him, but they didn't speak. He nodded and watched her walk by, marching along the path to the grotto and spring.

Smiling, he opened another cold beer.

Twenty minutes later, he heard her crashing through the underbrush on the south side of the house. He stood and leaned on the deck railing, waiting for her to emerge.

Red-faced and perspiring heavily, she stopped below him, leaned against a palm tree and mopped her face with the back of her hand.

"You're pushing it, you know," he commented pleasantly, taking a sip from the frosty can. "You've been very ill. Is all this running around really good for you?"

She swore, then leaned against the trunk of a coconut palm and closed her eyes. "I give up. Where is the damned street?"

"I told you. There aren't any streets on this island. There's no airport, no downtown, no boutiques, no craftsy shopping mall. There are no telephones, no television, no 7-Elevens, no mail delivery and no newspapers. There's no place to go. As of ten days ago, this island has a total population of two."

"Tell me you're lying," she whispered. "Please tell me that."

He gazed down at her. Heat pulsed in her face, and her legs trembled. She appeared ready to collapse.

"I think you've already figured out that I'm telling the truth." He spread his hands. "Welcome to Stone's Island, Miss James. What you see is what you get. Glorious isolation and solitude."

"Oh, God," she groaned, staring at him. "Are you serious? The most important story of my career and I can't phone it in?" She closed her eyes again and swayed. "And that's not the only problem." She had a big problem. Big. If only she could remember what it was. "Look, there has to be a way off this island. When does the next boat arrive?"

"If a boat shows up, it will be because the skipper lost his way. No vessels put in here on a regular basis."

"So how do I get off this island and back to civilization?" Her hands fluttered like small nervous birds, touching her lips, her hair, twisting together.

"You don't. You're stuck here."

"For how long?" she asked after a long silence. Her green eyes fixed on his face.

"The next supply plane won't arrive for another three months." A coldly satisfied smile curved his lips. Miss Caroline James was not going to blow the whistle on him anytime soon.

Abruptly Dax straightened and glared at her. Carrie James was not in this alone. He shared her dilemma. He was stuck with her, too. The realization appalled him.

Apparently she was no happier at the thought than he was. She muttered, "Three months," in a despairing groan, then her eyes rolled and she slid down the trunk of the palm in a dead faint.

Chapter Three

He was *fortunate* that she was a petite woman. Fortunate, too, that he was in good shape, since carrying Caroline James up the stairs and into the house was turning into a regular occurrence.

He deposited her limp body in the only chair that wasn't buried beneath stacks of paper, tilted her chin and moved her head back and forth until her eyelids fluttered open. She truly had the most remarkable eyes he had ever seen. Gazing into their translucent green depths made him feel instantly unsteady on his feet, as if he was being pulled down into mysterious whirlpools. He didn't like the feeling.

But he identified the source. The softly unfocused look in her eyes recalled to mind the satiny warmth of her skin beneath his palms, the sight of full, rounded breasts and the flare of her hips. He remembered noticing tan lines and imagining the shape of a brief bikini, remembered thinking how perfectly formed and lovely her body was.

Giving his head a shake, Dax stepped away from her, reminding himself that this woman had walked out of his door happily prepared to betray him. All

Carrie James cared about was her own selfish ambitions. He'd do best to remember that.

"I don't feel good," she said in a small voice. Bending forward, she pressed her forehead against her knees.

"If you're looking for sympathy, you won't find any here," Dax said coldly.

"Maybe it would help if I had something to eat," she murmured, talking to her knees. "I haven't had any solid food in days."

Pressing his lips together, Dax glared at her. In truth, she looked awful. Aside from the fact that her face and throat were peeling in sheets, as well as her arms, hands and legs, a tremor twitched across her shoulders and down her back. Her hands were shaking. When she lifted her face to give him a pleading look, he noticed how pale she was beneath the remnants of her sunburn.

"I'll fix you a sandwich," he muttered, walking to the kitchen area. Apparently his nursemaid days weren't over yet. Brooding, he shoved aside some dirty dishes to create space on the countertop.

He had come to this island to write. Instead, he'd lost ten days nursing a stranger whom he now knew he disliked. It angered him to remember how concerned he had been, how worried if he was doing the right things to help her.

And look how she repaid his care and anxiety.

Now he was stuck with her. Neither of them could leave the island. They couldn't escape from each other. How she would affect his life and his plans, Dax didn't know yet, but he could guess.

"What do you want?" he asked her, placing a can on the countertop. "Is Spam all right?"

Lifting her head from her knees, she cast him a look of distaste. "Well . . . actually, no." She placed a hand on her stomach and looked slightly sick. "Don't you have any tuna?"

Her picky attitude didn't bode well for their future together. Dax had no patience with fussy eaters. A person ate what was placed before her, and that was that. Moreover, guests did not criticize what the host offered. Aside from everything else that was wrong with Carrie James, and the list was growing, her manners needed improvement.

Grinding his teeth, Dax rummaged around for a can of tuna.

"I'm sorry," she said after a minute. Pushing out of the wicker chair, she walked to the counter on wobbly legs, brushed crumbs off a stool and sat down. "This isn't a very good beginning, is it?"

Ignoring her, he assembled the ingredients for a sandwich. Most of the bread was soggy and broke apart, but he managed to find two salvageable slices.

She frowned. "That looks appetizing."

"Do you want something to eat or don't you?" He glared at her across the counter and silently cursed the storm that had tossed her up on his beach. "I'm a writer, not a cook, okay?"

"Obviously," she said, her own voice sharpening. "You aren't much of a housekeeper, either."

"Look," he said, slapping down the can of tuna, "I didn't invite you here. And I don't need your sarcasm. The fact is, I came to this island to get away from people like you. You're intruding on my privacy and my hospitality. If you don't like what I have to offer, then you can climb back into your boat and sail out of here!''

Sunlight slanted through bamboo slats and glistened on the sudden moisture appearing in her eyes. "I didn't invite myself here, either," she said in a low, moist voice. "Right now I'm confused and upset. Discovering I'm stuck here is a shock."

"Oh, God." Dax shoved a lock of hair off his forehead. "You aren't going to cry, are you?"

"This situation is just..." She paused and drew a halting breath. "And you're not helping much. That was really a rotten thing you did, letting me think I could walk out that door and find civilization."

"I'd say you're in no position to make accusations." Flattening his palms on the counter, he leaned forward, anger tightening his chest. "You were going to sell me out. If you want my opinion, your snake editor is several notches higher on the evolutionary scale than you are!"

Her chin lifted. "Okay, you don't like me, and I'm not too crazy about you." The scab above her right eye gave her a slightly rakish appearance that deepened when she drew her lips down. "Are you positive there's no way off this island?"

"Believe me, right now I wish there was."

Reaching forward, she poked the sandwich as if to see if it were alive, then, apparently satisfied, picked it up.

"Why the publicity stunt? You know, a lot of your fans think you're dead, and they're very upset." Staring at him, she bit into the tuna, made a face and began to chew.

The question was laughable. "I came here looking for a little peace and quiet so I could work!"

She took another bite and considered his answer. "If that's true, then why didn't you just announce that you were going away for a while? Why the big mystery?"

"Because if I did, I wouldn't have had a moment's peace." At her scoff, he continued. "You think that's farfetched? It isn't! You can bet your press card that within two weeks, I'd have had a dozen boats out there and someone water-skiing up to my door."

She lifted an eyebrow.

"Believe it or not, fame has a downside," he said. "In my case fame means lack of privacy and countless intrusions. *That's* what this island is all about."

It suddenly occurred to him that she had managed to shift the focus off her low character and place him in a defensive position where he felt obligated to justify himself.

He began to glimpse the shape of things to come and he didn't like what he saw. She lacked scruples and gratitude, and she was going to be an albatross around his neck. He foresaw nothing but problems.

"Dax—may I call you Dax?—if there's no contact with the outside world, then where did you get this bread?" Easing back on the stool, she looked quite pleased with herself. She tilted her head and studied him as if blatantly accusing him of lying.

"If you had used the famed observation tactics of a competent reporter, you would have noticed a large garagelike building out back. And if you'd bothered to look inside, you would have seen the largest generator you've ever laid eyes on, and you would have noticed three commercial-size freezers. That's where the bread comes from. And the TV dinners we'll have later.''

"TV dinners," she repeated, drawing a breath. "Do you think TV dinners are healthy?''

"I feel fine,'' Dax said, grinding his teeth together. "Tell me you're not one of those health-food nuts. Because we're going to have a problem if you are.''

"I'm not a fanatic, but I believe it's important to maintain a balanced diet.'' An unhappy glance fell on her sandwich.

What amazed him was that someone in her position felt entitled to criticize. No man of Dax's acquaintance would have deliberately annoyed the benefactor on whom he depended for survival. But trust a woman to begin an unwanted relationship by trying to change him in the first five minutes.

Carrie ate the last bite of her tuna sandwich. "Thanks,'' she said, although she didn't look appreciative. "I wonder, is there anything to drink?''

"There's coffee, lemonade in the fridge, or tea if you want to make it. If you want something, help yourself.'' Dax decided he was through waiting on her.

"I think I will. But it's too cramped back there for both us. Would you mind getting out of the way?''

Irritation lifted his eyebrows. Now she was ordering him out of his own kitchen. But what could he expect? Carrie James had shown her true colors the minute she regained consciousness.

Frowning, he vacated the kitchen area and walked to the center of the room, turning to observe her.

Beneath her salt-stiffened shorts and wrinkled top, he could see the fluid movement of her small, lush body as she slid from the stool and moved behind the counter. Unconsciously Dax flexed his shoulders, watching the flash of long legs, exceptionally long legs for a petite woman. He recalled treating the cut on her thigh, remembered the smooth warmth of her skin.

Damn it! The last thing he needed or wanted was feminine distraction. He was having enough trouble writing as it was. Scowling, he rocked on his heels, crossed his arms over his chest and concentrated on how god-awful her hair looked plastered to her skull by sweat and sea water. She didn't smell all that appealing, either.

As for her face, he grudgingly conceded that she was attractive. Just how attractive was difficult to assess because of the scab over her eye and because she was still peeling. But there was no denying that she had great cheekbones and a clean, firm jawline. At the moment those magnificent emerald eyes dominated her features, fringed by long, sooty lashes that curled at the tips.

Gradually he made himself stop speculating about her appearance and became aware that she was slamming items around in his kitchen, disturbing the quiet he had come to cherish.

"There isn't a clean glass in this whole place!"

The accusation in her tone and gaze offended him. "If I'd known company was going to drop by, I'd have asked the maid to come in a day early."

"Look, I know I'm in no position to criticize—"

"Good. We finally agree on something."

She examined his expression. "But now that you bring it up, you've known you had company for ten days. You could have used that time to clean up a little. This place is a pigsty.''

''I was too busy taking care of an ungrateful stranger to worry about housekeeping! Something you need to keep in mind, Carrie, is the fact that this is *my* island, *my* house, and you're standing in *my* kitchen. If I choose to live unfettered by household chores, that is my choice.'' His eyes narrowed to slits. ''In case you haven't noticed, I'm really P.O.ed that you're here at all!''

Her eyes narrowed. ''I'm not too thrilled about it myself!''

''I went to one hell of a lot of expense and trouble to acquire this island and arrange the time to spend a year here. Now the isolation and solitude I went to all that expense and trouble to arrange is compromised because of you.''

''So what do you want me to do? Were you serious about me jumping back in the boat and rowing out of here?''

''Of course not.'' He stared at her, then shoved a hand through his hair. ''You know as well as I do that you aren't going anywhere. Unless you're some kind of navigational wizard, it would be suicide to put to sea in a boat that small.''

She cleaned a glass and poured lemonade into it, then slammed the fridge door with all her might. ''You know something? I'm starting to get mad.''

''No kidding,'' Dax said, walking to a window. He cast a moody gaze outside, focusing on an explosion of scarlet hibiscus.

''You're acting like I came here deliberately for the sole purpose of irritating you.''

"You *did* deliberately plan to sell me out. Am I supposed to like you for that?"

"Another thing…I'm not thrilled about waking up naked in a stranger's bed. Was that necessary?"

Dax felt her accusing stare burning against his bare back, bringing an uncomfortable flush to his throat and cheeks. "Your clothes were stiff and bloody. I needed to treat the cut on your leg, and it seemed reasonable to keep your skin cool and damp by sponging you. What was I supposed to do? Let you lay there in dirty clothes for ten days?"

Cursing under his breath, Dax realized he was doing it again. Defending himself. "How would *you* have treated a case of severe sunstroke?" he demanded, trying to focus the conversation back on her.

She ignored the question. "And it ticks me off that you seem to think I should be quivering with gratitude that you took me in. It seems to me you only did what any decent person would do. I've said thank you. What more do you want?"

"Is it too much to expect a little gratitude?"

"I should be grateful that I'm stuck on this island for the next three months." She shook her head and made a soft sound deep in her throat. "And with a man who looks and acts like a Neanderthal yet. Should I be grateful that I've lost my job? Grateful that Michael made a fool of me and wrecked my life? Grateful that my friends and family probably think I'm dead? And what's going to happen to my cat and my goldfish? Have you thought about that?"

"Are you suggesting that *I'm* responsible for your cat and your goldfish?"

"You can't even guess what being stuck here is going to do to my so-called life!"

Her voice was husky with moisture, and sudden tears swam in her eyes. "I'll lose my apartment, that's a given." Her lips trembled. "But it won't matter because my furniture will be repossessed when I'm not there to make the next payment. Which I probably couldn't do anyway because I no longer have a job. And by now my car has been impounded from the airport parking lot." A crystal drop slid down her cheek, followed by another. "Michael and I are finished, and that's not the worst of it by a long shot." There was something worse, if her mind would only let her remember.

She folded her arms on the countertop, dropped her head on top of them and sobbed, suddenly overwhelmed.

Dax stared at her, then cast a frantic glance over his shoulder, seeking help. He would have pledged next year's royalties to anyone who walked through his door right now and did something to make her stop crying. Sobbing women reduced him to helplessness. He didn't have a clue how to deal with a woman's tears.

Hating this situation, wishing he were a thousand miles away, he hesitantly approached the counter and gave her shaking shoulders an awkward pat while he searched for something comforting to say.

"Look, stop crying, will you?"

"Don't touch me!"

He jerked his hand back as if her shoulder blade had scalded him, then he thrust his fingers through his hair and gazed around the kitchen. The only thing he could think of was to feed her. "How about some more lemonade? Or another sandwich? Maybe I could find two more pieces of bread." It seemed to him that she just cried harder.

After shifting from foot to foot, he attempted another pat on her shoulder. "Listen...everything's going to be all right." Behind his beard, his lips pulled down in a grimace. What was he saying?

"It's not going to be all right! I need to get home!" Even her voice sounded wet, muffled by her arms. She really put herself into it. Her whole body shook with the force of her sobs.

Dax wet his lips and looked around for the roll of paper towels. When he found the roll, he nudged it against her arm. "Look, I'm sorry that I let you think you could find a phone," he said, hoping an apology might dry her tears. "You're right. That was a lousy thing to do."

"Yes, it was!"

That wasn't what she was supposed to say. She was supposed to accept his apology and forgive him so they could move on and she would stop crying. Feeling frustrated and helpless, Dax peered at her.

She looked tiny and pathetic, hunched over the counter. The sight of her made him feel like a brute. He had to remind himself that he had been received by the Queen of England. He had autographed a book for President Clinton. He had coached Julia Roberts and Mel Gibson through a scene in a film made from one of his novels, and afterward the three of them had gone out for dinner and drinks. In most circles Dax Stone was not considered an unsophisticated man. He was a man who could handle himself well in most situations.

Except when a woman burst into tears.

"Listen . . . why don't you lie down for a while, okay?" After a moment of fending off her slapping hands, he managed to pry her off of the counter. She clutched the paper towels against her chest and turned like she intended to lean against him, then she stared through swimming eyes at his beard, groaned and wobbled away. Dax couldn't decide if he was relieved that she hadn't sought comfort in his arms or faintly disappointed.

"Ordinarily I'm not a crybaby," she insisted, wiping at the tears that flowed freely down her cheeks. "It's just that so much has happened so fast, and it's all overwhelming. I mean my life is wrecked, absolutely wrecked, and there's nothing I can do about it because I can't get to a telephone and I can't get off this island." A deep sob convulsed her shoulders. "Mrs. Robinson, that's my next-door neighbor, she's taking care of Ringo, that's my cat, and Fannie Mae and Sheila."

"Fannie Mae and Sheila are your goldfish?" Dax hated it that he knew the names of someone's goldfish.

"Mrs. Robinson will probably keep them when I turn up missing, but she won't love them like I do . . . did."

Feeling like a clumsy oaf, Dax took her elbow and guided her toward the bed. "I understand," he murmured, lying. It was beyond his powers of imagination to believe that anyone could grieve the loss of goldfish.

"That's right," he said as she sank to the edge of the bed, covering her face in her hands. "Now lie back and rest. You've been very ill. I think you overdid it by running around the way you did."

Slowly, he backed away from the bed, stepping on papers and books. He was almost out of this situation. She wasn't making those awful sobbing sounds anymore. The crying had almost stopped. Maybe she would go to sleep.

He hadn't appreciated the calm and quiet during the time she was out of her head with fever and sunstroke. The part of his mind that seized on negatives whispered he had experienced all the tranquillity he was likely to find on this island. The arrival of Carrie James changed everything.

"I'll just work a while," he said, pointing to his computer. "After you've had a chance to rest, we'll talk. You tell me when you're ready."

God. She'd reduced him to babbling, to tiptoeing in his own house. He winced when his typing chair squeaked as he sat down, and he turned to check from the corner of his eye if the squeak had set her off again. He'd never figured out exactly what triggered a woman's tears.

When he saw that she was stretched out on the bed, staring at the ceiling through reddened, puffy eyes, he released a breath of relief and faced the computer screen.

Naturally, he couldn't work. His fingers rested on the keyboard like useless sticks.

It was impossible to concentrate on writing while he was straining to hear the next hitching breath from the bed and the next little hiccup, while he was dreading the thought that she might burst into tears again.

Dax contemplated his reflection in the blank monitor, then lifted his hands from the keyboard and combed his fingers through his mustache and beard. She had called him a Neanderthal.

Now that she'd planted the thought in his mind, that's what he reluctantly saw in his reflection. Not a heroic and manly vision of Robinson Crusoe, man against the elements. He saw a scruffy, oafish caveman with a bushy face full of fuzz. No wonder she fainted the first time she saw him. Leaning forward, he studied his reflection. He resembled a hedgehog.

"I'm sorry I fell apart," she said, speaking in a small voice.

"Try to remember this isn't the end of the world. Things could be worse." No wonder his recent chapters stunk, Dax thought, suppressing a groan. Every phrase was a cliché. "You could have died out there on the ocean, but you didn't. You have a roof over your head, and we have enough food for the duration." Before she could complain about Spam or TV dinners, he rushed on. "There's probably a blizzard raging in Denver, but here we have a sunny afternoon, bright skies and a temperature in the middle eighties."

"If you're advising me to count my blessings, thanks, but I'm not in the mood. Maybe when the shock wears off...." When he swiveled to look at her, she was still staring at the ceiling, her arms crossed over her breast like she was laid out in a coffin. "I wonder what Michael is thinking right now," she said after a silence.

"Michael. He's your snake editor, right?" Dax inquired politely, wondering if he was ever going to get any work done.

"Michael is the lying, cheating, lowlife attorney who swept me off my feet and then did me wrong."

"I see." It occurred to Dax that he didn't understand women at all. At this moment it utterly amazed him that he portrayed them well enough fictionally to ever have sold a novel. Why on earth would she care what Michael What's-his-name was thinking?

She rolled her head on the pillow and gazed at him out of tear-swollen eyes.

"Do you think Michael is worried? Do you think he's wondering what happened to me?"

A sigh lifted his chest. She looked so miserable and vulnerable that he found himself wanting to reassure her. He didn't know how this reversal of attitude had come about. But the bottom line was, whether he liked it or not—and he sure as hell did not—he and Carrie James were going to be living in uncomfortably close quarters for what he suspected would be a seemingly endless three months. As a practical man, he could see that it behooved him to move past his resentment and make an effort to get along with her.

"I'm sure Michael is going crazy with worry," he said finally, guessing that was what she wanted to hear.

"No, he isn't," she snapped, rolling her eyes toward the ceiling. She pressed her fingertips against her stomach. "I'll bet Michael's glad to be rid of me before his wife found out he was cheating. All I was to him was a problem. He's probably hoping I'm fish food and that I never show up again."

"I suppose he could feel that way," Dax said carefully. He was way, way out of his league when it came to dealing with the lovelorn. Relationships were not his area of expertise.

"Do you think so?" Sitting up, she leveled a stricken look at him. "Do you honestly think Michael is so rotten he could be *glad* I'm dead?" Fresh tears glistened in her eyes. "Okay, he said some hurtful things, but surely I meant *something* to him. We were seeing each other a couple of times a week for four months. How can you sit there and insist that he'd be glad if I were dead!"

"Hold it! Stop right there. I don't know this Michael. I have no idea what he might or might not be thinking!"

"Then why did you say he'd be glad to get rid of me?"

Dax had an impression he was bouncing around on an out-of-control merry-go-round. His brain spun, and he felt the beginning of a nasty headache. A reasonable man simply could not communicate with women. Women possessed a skewed form of logic utterly foreign to a man's comprehension. Women were not merely a different sex—they were a separate species.

"Look, Carrie, I didn't offer an opinion about Michael, you did," he said irritably. "And by the way, you shouldn't pick at that scab over your eye. It could get infected."

"I am so depressed," she said finally. "I need a shower and a mirror."

Dax studied her with a twinge of alarm. Given her present state of mind, the last thing she needed was a mirror. The minute she saw what she looked like, she was going to freak out.

"Why don't you rest first, take a nap," he suggested, frowning.

"Did you happen to find an overnight bag in the boat when you found me?"

"Sorry. I found some clothing on the beach, but no overnight bag." He watched her swing her legs over the side of the bed and look toward the bathroom door. "Seriously, why don't you rest awhile? You shouldn't overdo on your first day out of bed. You're already pushing it, don't you think?"

She gave him a long suspicious glare, then lifted her fingertips to her face. Flakes of peeling skin drifted around her. "My God," she whispered. Her hands flew to the hair plastered to her skull.

"Now, look, you aren't going to cry again, are you?"

"We've been talking all this time and I look like..."

Desperate, he glanced around for something to distract her. "Hey, Norman, old buddy." Standing, he rushed to position himself in front of the bathroom door. He waved a hand toward the parrot, who was preening himself in the sunlight. "Norman, this is our guest, Carrie. She needs something to make her smile. Do something, Norman." Norman ignored him. "Give him a minute," he said to Carrie. "Norman's a stitch."

"Please get out of my way." Her voice was thick and high-pitched, soggy with unshed tears. She pushed up from the side of the bed and turned toward the bathroom.

"Give Norman a chance, will you? You like animals, you're going to love Norman."

"Dax, please move aside."

He stared into her peeling face, then bolted across the room and hurried down the steps toward the beach.

He escaped just in time. From behind him came a blood-curdling scream. Norman flew out of the house right behind him.

Chapter Four

Carrie was the type who couldn't even wake up quietly. She awakened in fits and starts, tossing and stretching, murmuring and making little purring noises deep in her throat. Then, whatever she did in the bathroom, it required a lot of running water and banging sounds. And through it all, she hummed.

Dax was in no mood to play "Name that Tune." His body went rigid with irritation. When she finally emerged from the bathroom and padded toward the kitchen, still humming, he didn't turn from his computer screen. He was afraid of what he would do to her if he did.

But the interruptions continued.

First she inquired if he wanted some cereal and toast since she was fixing some for herself. Then she asked if she could borrow one of his shirts.

Dax's self-control snapped. He turned from his keyboard telling himself that he couldn't be held responsible for anything he did to her. But when he saw her, his chest tightened and the words died in his throat.

She stood before the door, munching a piece of toast and gazing toward the cove—wearing nothing but a bath towel.

Dax's mouth suddenly felt as dry as a desk blotter. After a minute he dragged his gaze away from the top of her thighs. Her long legs still looked sun pink, and the backs continued to peel, but those legs were gorgeously shaped, tapering along a curving line to slender ankles and small bare feet. An impression of soft, rounded lushness blindsided him. He stared at her and thought of strawberries and cream, of morning sunlight glowing on satin sheets.

Swallowing hard, he frantically tried to regain his anger and frustration, but his mind was firmly focused on sultry scenes involving showers and bath towels.

"I'm going to run a load of wash. I can't wear those shorts and that top the way they are. I've got the pink bikini bottom, but I need to borrow one of your shirts."

"What?"

When she turned around the sight of her took his breath away. The white bath towel covered the essential places, but also drew his attention to them. His imagination could readily supply what the towel concealed.

Fighting for control, Dax swallowed and fixed his gaze above her neck, concentrating mightily on the tumble of silky chestnut curls that framed her cheekbones. After her shower yesterday, he had noticed that her hair was honey brown, not dark, as he had supposed.

"It looks like I've got a wardrobe problem." Smiling almost apologetically, she shrugged prettily, the motion adjusting her cleavage. Dax bit the inside of his cheek and fought hard not to drop his gaze.

"Wardrobe," he repeated. The difficulty he experienced in following this conversation caused him to perspire.

"I have the clothes I arrived in, a bikini bottom and the dinner dress you found. That's it." She shrugged again, and Dax felt moisture on his brow. The rounded lushness of female flesh made the room seem several degrees hotter.

"Take whatever you need from my closet." He wrenched his eyes from her and focused on the ceiling.

"Thanks."

Blindly turning to his computer, he stared at the words on the screen without seeing them. The image of the towel wrapping her curves seemed burned on the retinas of his eyes. He could still see her long legs and the swell of her breasts.

"Dax?"

When he realized that she had called his name twice, he spun around in his chair and scowled. "Now what! I'm trying to work."

The annoyance in his tone had more to do with himself than with her, he thought guiltily. He didn't want her to guess how the sight of her jolted him, or that he had been abruptly reminded of her sexuality. And of his own.

To his relief, she had donned one of his blue cotton shirts and rolled up the cuffs. The tail hung to mid-thigh, leaving only a flash of pink bikini bottom and her long smooth legs to distract him, and an arrow-shaped wedge at the collar, which pointed directly to a deep shadowed cleavage. He swallowed, wondering if Carrie sensed the tension she was causing. An awareness of her physical presence bubbled through his blood like a sudden fever.

"Why did you decide on the name Norman? Was there a reason?"

"No." That was the truth, but right now she put him in mind of Norman Bates. He bit down hard with his back teeth.

She tossed bits of toast onto the deck, smiled as Norman hopped off the railing to inspect the offering. "Did you have a pet when you were a kid?"

A dazed look clouded his eyes, and he gave his head a shake. He could not believe he was sitting here discussing a parrot, for God's sake. If she had interrupted to ponder the meaning of life, or to speculate about a perfect paragraph, or to inform him that the house was on fire, that he could understand. But this trivia was making him crazy.

"Please don't interrupt," he snapped, swiveling to his keyboard.

Before he could type five words she started talking again. His shoulders slumped and he dropped his head.

"It really is gorgeous here. The air smells like perfume, don't you think? Do you know the names of the flowers?"

"Look, Carrie. I don't want to discuss your wardrobe, or Norman, or the scenery. I just want to work, okay?"

"Well, excuse me! I'm just trying to be sociable."

Positioning his fingers on the keyboard, he leaned forward to peer at the last sentence he had written, struggling to recall where he had been going with it.

"But you have to admit I've got a wardrobe challenge here." She frowned down at herself.

"Please! Could I please have some quiet?" he shouted. "I'm trying to work!"

"Okay, okay. I'm sorry. Geez."

A full ten minutes elapsed, and he began to hope she had gotten the message. No such luck.

"I think I'll go down to the beach and explore a little." She took one of his hats from a peg near the door and pushed it on her head. "Let's see. I've got my sunglasses. I found some sun block in the kitchen. Maybe I'll take—"

"Just go, okay? You don't have to talk about it." Dismayed, he blinked at the screen. He'd had a profound piece of dialogue in his mind. But it was gone now. Wait. He almost had it again. Dominique scans the place cards and says...

"Do you want another cup of coffee before I go?"

Dax threw up his hands. "No!" he roared. "What I want is some peace and quiet! Do you understand that? If you're going to go, go now!"

"I was just trying to be cordial. Maybe you ought to look that up in your dictionary!" The screen door banged behind her.

Remembering how she'd caught her shirttail in the door, Dax stretched his neck against his hands and smiled. Despite that rocky beginning, he'd ended by having the most productive morning he'd had in weeks. Finally the sentences had flowed, and Dominique's dialogue had sparkled.

Pushing away from the computer, he glanced at his wristwatch, then ambled toward the refrigerator, thinking about a Spam sandwich for lunch.

Stopping abruptly, he frowned and inspected his watch again, then lifted his head toward the beach. Carrie had been outside for several hours. Considering how tender the new skin emerging beneath the peeling must be, it could be dangerous for her to remain in the sun this long.

Suddenly worried, he banged through the screen door and rushed toward the beach, angry that he was forced to concern himself with someone else's problems.

THE BEAUTIFUL MORNING was followed by a beautiful day. Overhead the sky gleamed like a blue lacquer bowl, and the air felt like warm silk against Carrie's skin. Sunlight sparkled on long, foam-tipped waves that broke offshore, then rolled up a beach that reminded her of pale granulated sugar. The exotically shaped boulders that formed the arms of the horseshoe-shaped cove begged to be explored.

But not today. She didn't feel like exploring, after all.

Sitting beneath the shade of leaning palms, Carrie could imagine that she was the only person ever to set foot on this shore or to admire the profusion of flowering shrubs competing for space and sunshine at the top of the beach.

For several minutes she studied a tall tree dripping with dazzling yellow blossoms that streamed toward the ferns below like a shower of gold, wondering if she possessed the energy to collect some of the blooms.

No, she decided finally. All she wanted to do was sit here, drained by heat and depression, and stare at the horizon in hopes of seeing a vessel she could signal.

No ship appeared, but when she saw a jet stream arching overhead, she leapt to her feet and waved and hollered.

It was a dumb move. No one on the jet could see her.

Pulling her knees up under her chin, Carrie sat on the sand again and stared morosely at a collection of iridescent shells she had arranged in a line in front of her toes.

Three months was long enough that her cat and goldfish would transfer their affections to someone else. Ninety-two issues of the *Denver Post* would roll off the presses. She would miss three payments on her furniture. If the authorities didn't tow away her Jeep, she would owe the airport parking lot over seven hundred dollars when she returned.

By that time, Carrie's mother would have celebrated her fifty-third birthday, and her father would be three months closer to retirement. Big John, her kid brother, would have graduated from Colorado University. And she would not be there to share any of these events.

Michael would patch things up with his wife, maybe buy her an expensive bauble to assuage his guilt, assuming he felt any.

She eased a foot out from beneath the wet towels covering her legs and shoved one of the shells into the sand with her big toe, wishing it was Michael, she pounded it into the dirt.

It depressed her to realize that anger was all she felt when she thought about him. Ending the affair in such an ugly way didn't hurt like she thought it should have. Whatever she had felt for him had vanished in a poof of shock the instant she discovered what kind of man Michael really was.

But she had wanted to love him.

Sighing, Carrie fixed her gaze on the horizon. At twenty-eight, she was beginning to think she would never find the right man. When she met a good-looking straight guy with ambition and a sense of humor, he was either married or about to be married, or he was just divorced and it was too soon for a relationship, or he'd just moved in with someone and it was too late for a relationship. And he was either flat broke and had recently lost his job, or he had just been transferred to Calcutta, or he was only interested in blondes. There was always something. She had never been lucky with men. She laughed. Now there was an understatement. And now she was stuck with Dax— Mr. Congeniality.

"Carrie!"

Tilting her head to see beneath her hat brim, she watched the man himself run onto the beach. The muscles on his thighs and calves tightened and swelled as he stopped abruptly, then spotted her sitting beneath the shade of three palm trees. The low-slung cutoffs shifted on his hips as he strode toward her.

This was an absolutely knock-you-dead greatlooking man, Carrie thought, narrowing her eyes. That is, if you didn't count the awful beard. Today he'd pulled his hair into a ponytail, and that helped define his features.

He stopped a few feet from her and dug his bare heels into the sand. "You've been out here too long. You're going to get burned again."

"I'm fine. I'm sitting in the shade, I'm wearing a hat, your shirt covers my arms, and I've got wet towels over my legs."

Even though the breeze off the water made it cooler here than at the house, the midday sun was hot and they were both perspiring. Carrie noticed a damp gleam on Dax's shoulders, and tiny droplets glistened in the hair on his chest. The way he was standing, with one hip thrust slightly forward, shifted his cutoffs and she noticed a white strip where his tan ended.

She dropped her head and shoved another shell into the sand with her toe. "It's nice of you to be concerned. Surprising, but nice."

Irritation brought a rush of pink into her cheeks. Not two minutes ago she was thinking about Michael, now she was feeling attracted to Dax Stone, admiring his big, hard body through her large sunglasses. That Carrie could feel so powerfully attracted to Dax was further proof that her fleeting relationship with Michael had been only superficial. Or maybe the tropical heat was turning her into a nymphomaniac. She smiled at the thought.

"So how'd the writing go?"

"Pretty well, actually," Dax answered, sitting on the sand and leaning against a palm trunk. A faint note of surprise underlay his tone, but Carrie didn't pursue it. His work had probably gone well because she had left the house and come down to the beach.

They sat in silence, contemplating the watery horizon, both trying to think of something to say.

"I apologize for being so irritable earlier. I didn't mean to chase you out," Dax said finally. He didn't sound entirely sincere.

"You didn't chase me away. Coming down here was my idea." Raising a hand, Carrie touched the zinc oxide on her nose, realizing she probably looked goofy, a white nosed bundle wrapped in a tent shirt and towels. "I wanted some time alone to think."

Dax didn't say anything.

"I'm having a difficult time adjusting to the idea that I'm marooned on an isolated island with a stranger. Well, not a complete stranger, I guess. I know who you are, I've watched you on television interviews. But still." Wrapping her arms around her legs, she rested her chin on her upraised knees. "It's not a comfortable feeling to be totally dependent for shelter and food, for everything."

"I don't imagine it is."

His tone spoke volumes, reminding Carrie that she was dependent on the very person she had been prepared to betray. *Betray* seemed a strong word, but she sensed that was how Dax viewed it.

"I doubt you're any happier being stuck with a stranger than I am," she said after a minute.

He collected a handful of rocks and lobbed them toward the trunk of a palm. "Having you here changes everything. And not for the better."

Alarm made her heart skip a beat. "Is there a problem with supplies? Will we run out of food or something?"

"There's enough food in the storehouse to feed a dozen people for six months." He watched another stone ping off the palm trunk, then frowned at her. "I wanted a year to work on this book. Because of you, I'll only have three months."

For a moment Carrie was confused. When she understood, she ducked her head, feeling the heat in her cheeks. "Oh. Because the supply plane comes in three months. You figure I'll blow the whistle on you the minute I leave here."

"Won't you?"

She sat quietly, not looking at him.

"That's what I thought." His eyes blazed.

"Look, I'm a reporter. It's what I do—report the news. And you're news." She returned his stare. "We're never going to agree on this issue, so why don't we just call a truce? It seems like we have enough problems without worrying about what's going to happen three months from now." She spread her hands. "Maybe you'll finish the book you're working on by then and it won't matter. Who knows?"

"If I could write this book in three months, it would be finished now. And it damned well does matter!" Several strands pulled out of his ponytail when he thrust a hand through his hair.

"I could swear I read somewhere that you were a fast writer."

"This is a difficult project. I've wasted three months trying to get a handle on it. Now I'm starting over, plus I have to deal with your interruptions and all the noise you make."

"I'm sorry about the noise, but I can't spend the next three months tiptoeing and whispering."

"You could try to be considerate."

"And I will." Her chin came up and her eyes narrowed. "You can try, too." Before he could respond, she said, "It seems to me there's more to your disappearance than just wanting to write a book."

"Oh?" She felt his dark eyes burning on her.

"I guess I can understand that you might want to drop out of sight to work on a special project." She raised her head. "But what you're doing here could be dangerous."

"I beg your pardon?"

"I'm talking about not having a telephone or any other method of communication. What if you got sick? Or broke an arm or something? You could die here and no one would know. Didn't you think about that?"

"I had a ham radio when I arrived on the island. It's in the storehouse."

Hope leapt in Carrie's eyes. "Why didn't you say so earlier? We can radio for rescue!"

He shook his head, doodling in the sand with a fingertip. "It's inoperable. Originally the equipment was set up in the house." He looked toward the water. "I had an open can of deck sealant sitting on top. Norman got in the house and knocked the can over. Sealant ran into the radio. It hasn't worked since."

Carrie closed her eyes. For a moment . . .

"My arrangement with my agent was that if I ran into trouble, I'd call out on the ham radio. As a backup system, we agreed to a signal for the supply plane. If the pilot spots a blue flag on the flag pole, that's a sign everything is all right. If there is a red flag or no flag, it means I need help."

Carrie frowned. "If I remember what you said earlier, the next supply plane isn't due for nearly three months. Would it be correct to assume that you had a supply drop recently?''

"Right before you arrived.''

"So why didn't you signal that you needed help?''

He gazed at her. "I didn't need help.''

"Your radio is inoperable,'' Carrie said, spreading her hands in exasperation. "What if you break both legs tomorrow?''

"Then I'll be out of luck.''

"So this—'' she waved at the island "—isn't just about writing. It's also about man against the elements or some kind of macho stuff like that. Right?''

"I wouldn't phrase it quite that way,'' he said in a dry voice. Gathering his thoughts, he lifted a handful of sand and let it trickle through his long fingers.

"So how do you explain that you're willing to stay here with no hope of outside communication?''

He watched the sand mounding into a small pile beneath his closed palm. "Being marooned doesn't upset me the way it obviously upsets you. At this point in my life, I need to be alone. I prefer to be alone. For years I've been trying to meet other people's expectations, other people's deadlines, other people's agendas. Somewhere along the way, I lost sight of myself. Part of coming here was about finding myself again.''

Carrie studied his bearded face. "You couldn't figure this out at home?''

A harsh sound rumbled from his bare chest. "I barely had time to think, let alone analyze anything.'' He shook his head. "No, I needed to get away from people.''

"And now, here I come.''

His beard shifted in what might have been a rueful smile. "Now here you come."

Carrie adjusted her sunglasses. "I don't know how you stand the isolation. Don't you miss your friends?"

"Rarely."

"I already miss my friends. I guess I'm a people person."

"I'm not."

"I think I guessed that." She sighed. "You're different in person than you are on the TV talk shows."

"Oh?"

"On TV you seemed like a man who had it all together. You seemed confident, relaxed, like you knew exactly who you were and where you were going."

"Basically, I'd say that's true. I'm talking about a fine tuning, not a complete overhaul."

"In person you're bigger than I thought you'd be. Taller, bigger boned, bigger everything. And you seem like you're mad at the world."

Carrie recalled the interview she had watched on *Good Morning, America,* surprised by how vivid the memory was. She even remembered that Dax had been wearing a striped charcoal suit and a maroon tie. His hair had been thick and wavy and short, and he hadn't worn a beard. She had watched the interview, sighed and wondered why she never met guys that great-looking and that interesting.

"I'm sorry I happened to wash up on your shore," she said. "I'll try not to get in the way of your writing or your analyzing."

His eyebrows lifted. "I don't want you to get the wrong impression. I'm not anaylzing any who-am-I kind of crap. I know who I am. It's my professional life that needs examination, not my personal life. As for getting in my way, you're going to. Unfortunately we're living in uncomfortably close quarters.''

"True.'' Carrie gazed at the shells she was poking into the sand. God forbid that Dax Stone should have any personal problems. Macho men never did. "Have you ever lived with anyone before?''

"Once,'' he said shortly.

"It didn't work out?''

He stared at her. "No.''

When he didn't offer details, Carrie released a sigh. A reporter's instinct died hard. Or maybe she was just curious. Or nosy. Or maybe she had liked fantasizing that she was the first woman he had lived with. She had never been first for anything.

"For a short time I lived with a guy in college,'' she volunteered, although Dax hadn't asked. "And three years ago I let a man move in with me. That didn't work out, either.'' She sighed. "You really get to know someone when you live with him.''

They lapsed into an uncomfortable silence, Carrie's words hanging between them.

"I think we need to establish some house rules,'' Dax suggested finally.

A tide of depression overwhelmed Carrie. Three months. God. She waved a dispirited hand at a swarm of gnats busily investigating her hair. "I can guess the first rule. No interruptions while you're working.''

"I was hoping you'd understand.'' Relief softened his eyes to a golden amber.

"If I can't interrupt, I have to have free rein in the house.''

"Forget what I said about my island, my house, my things," he interrupted. "For our situation to work smoothly, you can't feel like a guest." He drew an unhappy breath. "You live here, too."

Unfortunately, Carrie thought, looking at nothing but blue sea all the way to the horizon.

"I'm a morning person—how about you?" Dax asked, obviously unhappy about having to work these things out.

"A night person."

"I eat an early dinner—do you?"

Carrie shook her head. "Late." As their preferences emerged, both of them started to look depressed. "As long as we're on the subject," she said, "is living with clutter and grit essential to your creative process, or would you mind if I cleaned up the torture chamber a little?"

He hesitated, studying her expression. "How much cleaning are we talking about?"

"A lot."

He stiffened. "Let's say I agree that we can use some housecleaning. You are absolutely not to move my papers or touch my desk. My desk is inviolate."

"I'll agree that your desk is off limits. But the rest... " Carrie shrugged and studied him through her dark glasses. Frankly, she hadn't expected him to concede so readily. This was an encouraging sign. "Why do you refer to your house as the torture chamber?" she asked curiously.

Standing, he moved out of the shade and took a few steps toward the water whispering up the beach. Sunshine gleamed on his bronzed skin, teased reddish highlights from his dark hair.

"Sitting in the house day after day reworking the same material is torture." After a minute he beckoned with his hand. "You really should go inside. If nothing else it's time you had some juice or tea. You need to drink a lot of liquids in the tropics."

Slowly Carrie rose to her feet and folded the towels over her arm. "It's really nice of you to worry about me," she said. "Coming down here to check on me and everything."

He looked dumbstruck. "I wasn't worrying about you." A faint shine of puzzlement appeared in his dark eyes. "Maybe I was." Instantly, he looked angry.

Carrie fell into step beside him, careful not to brush against him. "We'll both try to stay out of each other's way, okay?"

"Exactly." They walked toward the house, each pretending not to be especially aware of the other. "There's something else. I can't afford to keep jumping up and checking on you. The next time you go down to the beach, take my watch and don't stay in the sun too long. I have better things to do than be your nursemaid."

Carrie frowned. "I'm a big girl. I can take care of myself, thank you."

He slid a look toward her. "If you say so."

"You take care of yourself—I'll take care of myself."

They followed a row of fragrant oleander shrubs to the house, pausing beside the flagpole flying the bikini top. Dax rubbed his bearded jaw. "I found it on the beach. Is it yours?"

"Yes," Carrie said, glaring at the bikini top with barely concealed outrage. "I'd appreciate it if you'd take it down. I need every article of clothing I can get."

A dark flush spread beneath Dax's tan. Suddenly, putting the bikini top on the flagpole seemed like an adolescent thing to have done. He glanced toward the house and pulled his fingers through his beard. "About your cleaning project...."

"I can't wait to get started!" She could feel her spirits rise. Her life had been fast-paced and hectic. Waking up this morning with absolutely nothing to occupy her thoughts or time had sent her mood into a sinker. She needed to be active, needed projects to manage and complete. She needed to keep so busy and focused that she didn't have time to think about the future.

"You probably like to cook," Dax remarked unhappily, standing aside so Carrie could precede him up the stairs to the deck. "That's next, right? You'll start asking what I want for dinner."

"I enjoy cooking," she said briskly. "If you don't want me to ask what you want, then I'll cook what I like."

"You don't have to cook. TV dinners will suit me."

"So you said. But I don't like food that comes in little aluminum compartments."

She stepped inside the torture chamber and gasped at a sudden realization. "You don't have a television!"

"Television is a distraction."

"How can you live without watching the news?" Even people who hated TV watched the news. "What if an earthquake leveled the United States," she asked, staring at him. "We wouldn't know it!"

"That's the point," he explained patiently. "I don't want to know. We couldn't do anything about it, anyway."

Carrie thought a minute. She planted her hands on her hips and tilted her head. "You're a Republican, aren't you?"

Right away he understood the direction of her thoughts. "And you're a Democrat."

"I'll bet you hate parties."

"And you love them."

"You'd rather have your fingernails ripped off than go shopping."

"You were born knowing how to find the smallest boutique in the biggest mall."

"You love football."

"And basketball."

"I hate sports."

Dax sighed. "I wonder why I'm not surprised."

A rueful smile curved Carrie's lips. "Talk about the odd couple. It's a good thing we only have to put up with each other for three months." Still thinking about their differences, she tilted her head and gazed at him. "At least we both like to read. Who's your favorite author?"

"It's a toss-up. Dean Koontz or Stephen King. And yours is ... Let me guess." He pursed his lips and examined the dusting of freckles that sprinkled her cheeks and nose. "Danielle Steel?"

"Wrong." She gave him a coy smile as she brushed past him and entered the house. "My favorite author is Dax Stone. I've read everything he's written."

Dax stopped in his tracks, dumbfounded.

Chapter Five

Dax paused over his keyboard and watched Carrie from the corners of his eyes.

She was down on her hands and knees, attacking the wood floor with a scrub brush that she wielded like a weapon. Every once in a while she sat on her bare heels, and with the back of her hand, pushed a tumble of curls away from her flushed face.

And what a face it was. The pink of exertion glowed on her cheeks. Sunlight slanted across the delicate lines of her cheekbones and throat.

It occurred to Dax that Carrie James was one of the few women he knew who looked beautiful without makeup. Her mouth was well shaped and naturally rosy. Her brows and lashes were a silky color only a shade lighter than her hair. Far from appearing pale or pallid, she had a healthy cheerleader glow about her. For some reason he equated freckles with cheerleaders. It wasn't an unflattering image. He hoped she didn't cover the freckles with makeup when she dressed to go out.

For a moment his thoughts drifted, visualizing her dressed in something low-cut and clinging—like the green cocktail dress he'd found—wearing dark nylons that hugged the curves of her legs.

"It's coming along, if I do say so myself," Carrie said in a satisfied voice, breaking into his reverie.

"It looks good," he agreed politely, though he wondered if he referred to the floor or to the image of her in his daydream.

"This job isn't as obnoxious as I thought it would be. The exercise feels good." She dipped the brush into a bucket of soapy water. Dax wondered where she had found the bucket. He didn't remember listing one on the supplies inventory.

She shook the brush over the bucket, then leaned over to the floor. It seemed to Dax that she moved in rhythm to a sultry song that only she could hear.

Swallowing hard, he watched her a full minute more, then returned to his keyboard. And he wrote the hottest sex scene he'd ever produced.

HE SAT HUNCHED OVER the computer, flexing one shoulder, then the other. The motion sent a ripple of muscles flowing across his broad bare back. When he straightened, he rolled his head slowly from one side to the other.

The sight of swelling muscles and tendons was too much for Carrie. She turned away and bit her lip. He'd been doing that all day, and she'd almost memorized every ridge and bulge on his back and shoulders. If she didn't get away from the house and away from Dax, she was going to explode. She couldn't recall ever being so physically aware of any male.

"I think I'll go for a run on the beach." She stood abruptly and wiped her brow. She was flushed and perspiring—and she suspected it wasn't entirely from the physical exertion.

"Good idea. Mind if I join you? A run would feel good, help loosen the kinks."

Yes, she did mind if he joined her, but she didn't say so. She draped a towel around her neck and stepped toward the door, bumping into him as they both tried to exit at the same moment.

Face burning, she hurried past him when he stepped aside with a murmured apology, angry that her skin tingled where she'd pressed against his hard naked chest. Why couldn't he ever wear a shirt?

She shooed Norman off the deck. "That's one cheeky parrot. He'd demand his own place at the dinner table if we'd let him."

Dax followed her down the steps, then stopped abruptly and peered at his flagpole. "Where'd you find a red towel?"

"In the storehouse out back." She continued down the path. "In case the supply plane comes early, I want the pilot to see a red distress signal."

Distress was right. Judging from the pace her pulse was keeping, she needed to be rescued—and fast.

Dax remained silent until they emerged at the top of the beach. "Carrie, the plane isn't going to come early. Don't get your hopes up."

She walked to the edge of the water and let the froth of a wavelet swirl around her ankles. "You never know. It seemed like a good idea to put up a red flag."

The breeze felt wonderful blowing off the water. Carrie lifted her face and breathed in the salty air. The different scents of the island fascinated her. Near the water she couldn't smell the heavy fragrance of blooming shrubs and flowers or the rich, earthy odor that overhung the mossy area near the spring and grotto.

"It's cooler here. It was getting too hot in the house," she murmured. Lord, that sounded suggestive. "I wish you'd installed air-conditioning." The rush of the surf smothered the sound of footsteps, but she knew instantly when he moved up behind her.

"I wanted to keep things as natural as possible." He paused. "It does seem hotter than usual."

Carrie flushed. "Maybe the seasons are changing or something."

When he laughed, Carrie straightened and blinked at him in surprise. She hadn't heard him laugh before.

"I never imagined I'd be standing on a twilight beach talking to a beautiful woman about the weather."

He thought she was beautiful? The knot in her stomach twisted tighter. She rubbed her hands together in a nervous gesture. "I'll race you to the rocks." If she didn't release some of the tension bubbling inside, she was going to fly apart.

"What does the winner get?" he inquired in a light, bantering tone, then instantly looked appalled as if he wanted to withdraw the question.

Carrie hated it, but everything either one of them said made her think about sex. She'd spent the whole day thinking about sex. She wet her lips.

"I don't know. What do you want?" Oh, God. She was making it worse. She tried to smile and salvage the moment. "What would make a worthwhile prize?"

"Something good to eat." Fiery color burned upward from his throat. "You know, dinner."

"You'll get that anyway." Was sex inevitable? Was that what she was saying? Face burning, feeling confused, Carrie threw up her hands, then dashed down the beach, running as hard as she could.

A moment later Dax drew up next to her her, running flat out, his head down. When he passed her, his arm brushed hers, and a thrill of electricity shot through her body that almost made her stumble. Clenching her teeth, she focused straight ahead and continued running, feeling her lungs start to burn.

She honestly could not figure out her growing attraction to Dax Stone. He resented her being on the island. He was about as amiable as a cactus. They were not together because they wanted to be, and they had next to nothing in common. Yet Dax Stone exuded a powerful masculine appeal, and she responded to it.

It wasn't only that he was sexy as hell and had a fabulous body, although Carrie was increasingly aware that he did. Her fascination also had to do with his prickly personality and the fact that he lived in a world similar to hers but different.

Dax Stone was a serious and successful novelist, whereas Carrie had never been more than a hack. She could dash off an article detailing who, what, when and where. But she knew in her heart that she lacked the talent to plot or write a novel, and sustained periods of in-depth concentration left her feeling physically and emotionally drained. Whereas Dax emerged from such bouts looking invigorated and fresh.

It was as if he withdrew into a visionary world within his mind that was as real to him as the world he seemed to shut out. Watching him at his computer was like watching a mystic in a trance, tapping out clues on the keyboard.

When they reached the boulders that formed one arm of the cove, they leaned against an altar-shaped rock and mopped their faces with the towels around their necks. "How's the writing going?"

Immediately he bristled and his expression closed. "I don't like to discuss works in progress."

Carrie shoved back her curls and turned her flushed face to the breeze. "I'm pretty good at critiquing. Terry used to say I'd probably have been a better editor than a writer."

Alarm flared in his thick-lashed eyes. "Look, Carrie. My work is absolutely off limits. I don't need your input, don't want your opinion. Do you understand? I work alone."

She shrugged. "Suit yourself. I'm just trying to be helpful." Plus, she was dying to read the latest Dax Stone novel. "This is my favorite time of day," Carrie said, changing the subject. Periods of silence unnerved her, made her acutely aware of him. A brilliant sunset fanned across the horizon as the sun skimmed the tops of the waves. Orange and pink and tinges of scarlet flared against indigo. "That's the bad part about living in a city. You don't get to see sunsets like this."

"I can think of things about city living that I'd describe as worse than missing sunsets."

She studied his face, hating the shaggy beard. "I can't tell if you're smiling or not."

Her comment seemed to please him. "I have a theory about beards being prevalent in closed societies and less favored in open societies. Maybe I was born in the wrong age. I don't like people trying to guess what I'm thinking.''

"Hiding, huh?"

He stared at her. "No."

"In my opinion, you'd look better without all that hair," she said, trying to sound tactful.

"I like it," he said defensively. "I think a beard gives me a slightly menacing look."

Her eyebrows rose. "Why on earth would you want to look menacing?"

"Horror writers ought to look a little menacing, don't you think? My publisher certainly does. I think Ken half believes that anyone who writes about vampires probably knows a few personally."

"I've wondered about that myself," Carrie said, laughing. She touched his arm, felt the rock hard-muscle there and hastily withdrew her fingertips. "Nevertheless . . . I think the beard ought to go. But hey, mine is just one opinion. I don't want to be pushy or anything. Don't shave on my account."

Now it was Dax's turn to look surprised. "That never entered my mind." He paused, studying her. "As for pushy . . . it's been my experience that report-ers are the pushiest people on the planet."

"You're right." Carrie smiled at him. "Okay, shave that ugly thing off. Is that pushy enough for you?"

His laugh was wonderful, deep and genuinely amused. "Can't get much more pushy than that."

"That was nothing. You should have seen me when I was hot on the scent of a story."

The sun's dying rays slanted across his face, turning his gaze into a kaleidoscope of golden browns and amber. "I did."

"Oh." Carrie shifted uncomfortably. "I forgot." Changing the subject again seemed like a good move. "What makes this book so special anyway, that you need a whole year to write it?"

Dax considered her for a second, quiet, then he raised both hands and pushed his hair back. "Let's talk about you. Did you grow up in Denver? Is that where your family lives?"

"My home town is Memphis, Tennessee, but we moved to Denver when I was thirteen. My dad is with IBM, which, as everyone knows, stands for I Been Moved. My parents live in Galveston now."

"Any siblings?"

"A brother who is about to graduate from CU." She smiled, seeing John in her mind. "He's as much of a slob as you are. You should see his room at the frat house." Leaning against the warmth of the rock, she gazed at him. "How about you? Where is your family?"

"My parents are dead. I have five brothers and sisters scattered around Massachusetts and Delaware."

"You come from a large family?" That surprised her. Dax Stone seemed like such a loner that Carrie couldn't imagine him surrounded by family.

"Yes."

Something flickered in his dark eyes. Regret? Nostalgia? Carrie couldn't identify what she saw. But she was fairly certain that he didn't realize it when he lifted a hand and smoothed a tendril off her cheek, tucking it behind her ear. His unexpected touch jolted her into paralysis, but he didn't seem to notice.

"And they're all married. I've got eight nieces and nephews."

Carrie's cheek tingled where his fingertips had touched, as if he had left a mark there. With difficulty she resisted an urge to raise a hand and explore the spot herself. Aware of the sudden awkward silence, she groped for something to say. "So, where are you in the birth order?"

"I'm the youngest."

She forced a smile. "Then we should get along fine. Not too long ago I read that the best combination is a firstborn daughter and a youngest son."

He looked at her with an unreadable expression. When Dax looked at something, he focused his entire attention on that something. Carrie gazed into his dark eyes and felt an electric jolt of connection. For a moment she almost believed that he was looking directly into her thoughts and mind, examining her secrets. That made her uncomfortable. There was one secret that not even she could face. If only she could remember what it was.

"That's what the book said," Carrie remarked, suspecting she was babbling. "The firstborn daughter is a manager, used to taking care of those who came after her."

"A controller."

"I suppose you could say that. While the youngest son is accustomed to everyone babying him and taking care of him. You can see how a couple like that would mesh."

One eyebrow lifted. "Why, Miss James, are you proposing?"

"Of course not." Crimson flooded her cheeks. "I'm just saying it's kind of interesting, that's all."

"I don't see myself as needing or wanting to be babied. I'm not looking for a woman to mother me."

They were standing close enough that Carrie saw the heat in his eyes, saw a sudden intensity that made her heart pound and her mouth go dry.

For the first time she realized that she wasn't the only one struggling with strange yearning thoughts. There were two people on this romantically isolated island, two sets of appetites and hungers. There were two healthy, red-blooded adults coping with the sight of bared flesh and the intimacy of living in close contact.

Suddenly she remembered his hands on her naked body, gently smoothing burn lotion across her throat and chest, along the curve of her legs and thighs.

Her eyes dropped to the sweat glistening on his chest. In the lavender light of approaching evening, his taut skin looked smooth and inviting. She experienced a sudden crazy urge to spread her fingers across his shoulder muscles.

"We'd better go back," she said in a throaty voice. Quickly, lest he misunderstand, she added, "I have a roast in the oven."

But she didn't move. Helplessly she stood in front of him as if his body was a magnet binding her within the radius of his heat and vitality. And she imagined she could see electricity flashing from her skin to his, tingling over them both.

"A roast?" he asked, his voice husky. His gaze dropped to the tremble that had begun at the corner of Carrie's lips. "Pink in the middle?"

She wet her lips and nodded, feeling the magnetic tug of his body. He stood with his thighs apart, his cutoffs low on his hips. If Carrie lowered her gaze, she would see the dark arrow of crisp curly hair disappearing into his shorts, reappearing at the top of his thighs. Thinking about what lay between made her feel dizzy and shaky inside.

"You have remarkable eyes, did you know that?" he said suddenly. "I've given some of my characters green eyes, but I don't think I've ever actually seen green eyes before. In this light, your eyes remind me of emeralds."

Carrie lifted a shaking hand and placed it on her chest. If her heart beat any faster, she was going to faint.

The thing that saved her was a suspicion that he was about to kiss her. At that moment Carrie wanted him to kiss her as much as she had ever wanted anything. But a kiss would open them to complications she didn't even want to think about. Still, she felt herself sinking beneath the spell of warm island breezes and glowing sunset, the resonance that sang between male and female.

She stumbled backward a step. "The roast," she said vaguely, waving a hand. "I know you like to eat early...."

"The roast," he repeated in that same husky tone. His dark eyes traced the contour of her lips. "Are you cooking a roast?"

"Yes." She thought she had already mentioned that, but she wasn't sure. The last few minutes had scorched her mind. Turning, feeling shaky inside, Carrie bolted away from him, jogging along the curve of the shore.

Dax fell into step beside her. When his arm brushed hers with a jolt of heat lightning, they both stopped, unaware that water bubbled around their ankles.

"You don't have to cook," he said, staring at her. "We have the TV dinners."

She wished she could see his mouth. "TV dinners are full of preservatives."

"What kind of preservatives?" His gaze traveled across her hot cheeks and settled on the hollow at the base of her throat.

"I have no idea," Carrie whispered. If she took one step forward, she would be in his arms. The heat of his body surrounded her, drew her forward. She could almost stand under his chin.

"Me, either." He noticed that the hollow at the base of her throat throbbed with her pulse. He watched, and his shoulders tightened.

"We'll have to find out." Her breath emerged in erratic spurts, coming too quickly, then stopping altogether.

"Definitely."

Carrie rubbed the goose bumps that had appeared on her arms despite the warm night air. "We're talking nonsense," she said, sounding a little wild even to herself. "Come on, I'll race you back to the house." Spinning, she took off at a run, her heart pounding.

IT WAS ALMOST A RELIEF to discover a problem when they reached the house, Dax decided. Anything to take their minds off those intensely erotic moments on the twilight beach. He didn't understand precisely what had happened. One moment they had been talking, the next moment all he could think about was her mouth and how she would taste if he leaned forward and kissed her.

"I'm sure I left a light on," Carrie said, halting beside the flagpole.

"It was probably operating the oven for so long."

"I'm sorry, I don't understand."

"The house is largely powered by solar energy. Running the oven for a couple of hours must have drained the batteries."

The last dying rays of sunset reflected in her eyes when she lifted her face. "What do we do now?"

Her sunburn had faded to a golden sheen that made Dax think of antique gold and ivory. The perfect setting for emerald eyes. "I have a backup generator in the storehouse, remember? If I can't fix whatever's going on, we'll use that. I'll get a flashlight and be back in a couple of minutes."

He left her standing on the deck facing the cove, her face bathed in a sunset glow. Frowning, he turned and followed the dancing light of the flash up the path to the storehouse.

Usually he considered fiddling with the generator an annoyance, but now he welcomed the chore. It gave him time to think about what had happened on the beach.

He had looked down into Carrie James's face and suddenly he had wanted her like he had wanted no other woman. The memory of her naked body beneath his hands had overwhelmed him. He had been standing close enough that he could smell the apricot fragrance of her hair and the clean, fresh scent of her skin.

A steamy warmth continued to radiate from her several minutes after their run along the shore, and his body had responded strongly to her womanly heat and to the mingled scents that he was beginning to identify as hers alone.

Stepping into the storehouse, he checked the generator, then swore. This was going to be an all-night job.

Maybe that was best. Right now he didn't trust himself with Carrie.

After finding his toolbox, he placed the flashlight on a shelf, aiming the beam of light at the generator, then started tinkering.

The question that bothered him was whether it was Carrie James who had aroused his desire, or if he would have experienced the same strong reaction to any woman who appeared on his island. It had been a long time since he'd taken a woman to bed.

Suddenly Laura rose in his memory. He saw her the way she had been a year ago, the last time he had seen her, crying and angry, throwing her things into the big brass chest that she called her hope chest. Helpless in the face of her tears, he hadn't answered when she shouted that she was tired of competing with a damned computer, that she wanted to be needed and Dax didn't need anyone. Most important, Laura wanted a baby and a man who could give her one. Embarrassed and feeling like a failure, he had hightailed it out of there. From that moment he'd started thinking about getting away from everything.

Was it getting away or running away? he asked himself. Getting away, he replied with a scowl.

Leaning against the generator, Dax scrubbed a hand over his eyes and down his face. A year was a long time without the intimacy of a woman's soft warmth and laughter. Oddly, he hadn't thought much about it until Carrie James washed up on his beach.

Odder still, during the time he was treating her sunburn, rubbing the lotion on her naked body, he was aware of her nakedness and her beauty of form, but seeing and touching her had not been an arousing experience. It was arousing only in retrospect, now that he knew a little about the woman inside that magnificent body. Now the memory of her warm curves beneath his hands made his chest tighten and his body stir.

But he didn't understand why he was beginning to think of Carrie as the sexiest woman he had ever met.

Certainly she was not a flirt. She didn't flaunt her sexuality, as Laura had done. And she didn't go out of her way to impress or please him. Not to mention they had next to nothing in common.

On the other hand, he suspected that Carrie James was like a cat—she would always land on her feet and cheerfully go about adjusting to whatever circumstances she found herself in. Although he hated it that she was prepared to sell him out, he couldn't help admiring her honesty.

Aside from a moody first few days, she was generally positive and seemed to have a happy nature.

Moreover, she was a considerate person, and willing to compromise.

Plus—and this continued to amaze him—Carrie James had read all his books—even *Live Bait,* his first, which damned few people had read and fewer had had the courage to criticize, including his agent. Not Carrie. She had told him right to his face that it was lousy.

"Dax? Can you fix the generator?"

He started as he heard her stumble into the dark storeroom. "Go ahead and eat without me," he growled. "This is going to take a while."

She was quiet for a minute. "Do you want me to stay and keep you company?"

That's the last thing he wanted. He wouldn't be able to concentrate on what he was doing. "Thanks for offering, but I'd rather know that roast isn't going to waste. Leave me a plate on the counter, will you?"

After a minute he heard her leave, and he rocked back on his heels, staring into the darkness.

Carrie James possessed many remarkable qualities. But he wished she had never come into his life.

THE NEXT MORNING he swung his legs out of the hammock, stretched, then padded inside, passing Carrie on his way to the coffee machine in the kitchen.

She lay sleeping on her side, wearing one of his shirts. A halo of chestnut curls framed the smile on her lips. Her cheeks were slightly flushed, forming a pretty contrast to the fringe of dark lashes that curled on her cheekbones.

He peeked at her again on his way to the bathroom, wondering why a woman looked so sexy when she wore a man's shirt. Or why it was that a foot poking out of a sheet could seem so vulnerable and endearing.

Shaking his head, he stepped into the bathroom, set his coffee mug on the edge of the sink and examined himself in the mirror, turning his face to one side, then the other.

Perhaps his experiment with the beard had run its course. Actually a beard was itchy. He'd certainly feel cooler without it. And lately he'd been concerned about catching food in the mustache.

As he searched for his razor, Dax listed every reason for shaving except the one that actually motivated him to squirt shaving cream into his hand, then rub it into his cheeks and fuzzy chin.

Carrie James didn't like beards.

Chapter Six

"You shaved!"

Carrie sat up in bed and opened her eyes to the sight of a new Dax carrying a mug of steaming coffee. She blinked and stared, wondering if she was still dreaming.

Without the scruffy beard Dax looked like a different person. Now she saw a strong, stubborn jawline and a firm chin. His mouth was wide and well shaped, a poet's mouth capable of humor or subtle cruelty. Now she had a better perspective of his nose, which was straight and long with a patrician thinness.

She gaped at him. Dax Stone was simply the most ruggedly handsome man Carrie had seen off a film screen.

"Don't get any ideas," he said immediately. "I didn't shave because some pushy reporter suggested I should." Raising a hand, he stroked his chin with a self-conscious gesture and gave her a thin defensive smile. "I feel naked."

"I know you didn't do it for me," Carrie said—though she couldn't help but wonder a little. "I like you better this way nevertheless. You look wonderful.'' And he smelled good, too. A faint but clean and intoxicating scent of after-shave wafted toward her as he passed the bed.

He shrugged and sat down at his desk, but Carrie saw him inspect his reflection in the screen before he turned the computer on.

Hiding a smile, she pulled down the hem of the shirt she had borrowed to sleep in. By now she knew Dax was fiercely protective of his autonomy and did not welcome any encroachment. But she also knew he wasn't nearly as prickly as he wanted her to think.

The image he projected on TV, and in real life, too, was that of a strong loner who didn't care what other people thought. Confident, self-sufficient, an island unto himself. Dax Stone did what he wanted to do when he wanted to do it, and to hell with the rest of the world. He was impervious to outside opinions and conventions.

Except Carrie sensed that he wasn't. She sensed that beneath that hard shell was a lonely man who yearned for approval and acceptance just like everyone else.

She slid her legs over the side of the bed, stretched and yawned, running her fingers through her hair.

''My dad had a beard once. For about six months. But my mom didn't like it, so he shaved it off.''

''I told you, I didn't shave for you. I shaved because I wanted to.'' Leaning forward, he peered at the computer screen.

''My brother wears a mustache, but I think that's only a phase. You know, to see how he looks. He'll probably shave after he graduates and starts looking for a job.''

"Carrie... I'm trying to work." His fingers tapped at the keyboard.

She went into the kitchen for coffee but Dax had left only a few drops. "You drink too much coffee," she commented, rinsing out the pot and looking out the window at another gorgeous day. "That isn't good for you. You should drink water instead. Everybody should drink more water. You want some?"

"What I want is some quiet," he growled. "So please shut up."

"And it worries me that you don't always eat breakfast. Breakfast is the most important meal of the day." She shook some vitamins into her hand and went over to him. "If you aren't going to eat right, you can at least take vitamins. Here, take these."

He threw up his hands, then swiveled to glare at her. "If I take those, will you stop talking?"

"Probably not." She gave him a bland smile and thrust out her palm. "You can be as moody and snappish as you want, but you aren't going to spoil my day."

"Oh, for God's sake. Give me the damned things." He took the vitamins and the glass of water she held out, glaring at her legs beneath the hem of the shirt-tail. "Why are you so revoltingly cheerful all the time? Sometimes I think I liked it better when you were sick."

"Why are you so angry all the time?"

He stood up and leaned forward, towering over her. "I came here to get away from people and interruptions and distractions. To write. Not to clean or defend my eating habits. I never dreamed I'd be sharing a bathroom with a woman or giving up my bed or keeping *you* company!"

Carrie drew herself up and leaned forward, too, stretching up on her tiptoes until they were almost nose to nose. "Hold it right there. I don't need to be entertained. I can amuse myself, thank you very much."

"Oh, come on. You're bored, admit it."

"Me? Bored?" She blinked in genuine astonishment. "I've never been bored in my life! Do you see those papers on the bedside table? Those are lists. What I want to do after I'm rescued, jobs I might enjoy, things I have to do when I get home."

"Whenever I work, I feel you looking at me! Like you resent it that I'm not talking to you."

"Don't flatter yourself, buster. Sure, I like a little conversation occasionally, but—"

"We have conversation every minute of every hour, to my everlasting regret!"

"But I can get along without it, too! So, if you want to work, feel free!"

"Good. That's exactly what I want to do!"

"Fine."

Turning smartly on her heel, her chin in the air, Carrie marched to the kitchen, opening and slamming the cabinet doors, not sure what she was looking for. Dax sat heavily in his chair and stared at the screen.

"*You know,*" she said, picking up their conversation after she had showered, dressed and calmed down, "until you mentioned it, I didn't think about taking your bed. I apologize for being inconsiderate. I should have thought about this sooner."

Dax dropped his head and shook it, his hands going limp on the keyboard. "You are driving me crazy. You never stop talking. I have never met anyone who talks as much as you do."

"I guess I thought you preferred the hammock."

"I love the hammock. I'm wild about it. Discussion closed, all right?"

"You brought this up," she reminded him, throwing a glare in his direction.

"And I deeply regret it." He scowled at her. "I don't care if you have the bed."

"I could sleep in the hammock. Or we could trade off."

"I was angry, just talking off the top of my head. Forget about the bed."

"I'll take the bed for a week, then you take it and I'll move to the hammock." She frowned, thinking about it. "Except what happens if it rains? There's no roof over the hammock."

"Carrie, please...I don't care if you have the bed."

"Are there any wild animals on this island? I mean, is that something I should worry about when it's my turn to sleep on the deck?"

He jumped out of his chair, crossed to her in three long strides, pulled her into his arms and kissed her hard and furiously.

Her surprise bordered on shock, and she stiffened, her hands rising to his chest to push him away. But she didn't. The instant his hard, demanding mouth came down on hers, Carrie felt an electric jolt shoot through her body. It began at the top of her scalp and shot down like a hot arrow, pinning her to the floor.

Heat was the primary sensation. A thrilling explosion of feverish heat enfolded her as his arms tightened around her body, and crushed her against his chest. She felt the bigness of him, the animal fire radiating from his large body to hers, and it paralyzed her. She could not have stepped away from him if the fate of the world had depended on it. Instead of pushing him away, her fingers tangled in the hair on his chest, and she clung to him, returning the hard, angry pressure on her lips.

When Dax released her mouth, he stared at her. Carrie had no difficulty reading the surprise in his expression, followed by a rush of embarrassed discomfort.

"I'm sorry," he said in a thick voice. "I just wanted to shut you up, and . . ." His voice trailed as if he had forgotten what he intended to say. And he seemed to have forgotten that he was still holding her in his arms.

But Carrie had not forgotten. She felt his arousal, hard and firm against her stomach, making her feel weak inside and fluttery. Never in her life had she been kissed with such intensity. Never before had she felt as small and helpless or as powerfully attracted to a man. It was as if some kind of body chemistry existed between her and Dax Stone that she had not encountered with any other man, something powerful and wildly exciting.

"It's all right," she whispered. Her voice sounded husky, sort of like Kathleen Turner in the midst of a seduction scene. "I know I talk too much. I can't help it. I don't mean to interrupt, the words just come out."

The imprint of his kiss lingered on her lips, tasting of morning coffee and faintly of orange juice. His chest felt rock-hard beneath her fingertips. She tried to ignore the pressure against her stomach, but it made her feel weak-kneed and melting inside. She was acutely aware that it was only a few steps to the bed, aware that they were two healthy adults experiencing a sudden and searing desire for each other.

Nervously, she licked her lips and held her breath, waiting to discover what would happen next. Part of her urgently wanted Dax to sweep her into his arms and carry her to bed. Another part resisted the complications sex would inject into their tenuous relationship.

Dax seemed to finally notice that he was holding her molded against his hard body. He dropped his arms to his sides and stepped back, swallowing.

"I apologize. I had no right to do that."

"It's all right, I understand." Carrie waved a hand, the motion awkward. Apparently he didn't want additional complications, either. "Look, I think I'll take the rubber boat out. Into the cove. Maybe I'll catch us a fish for dinner."

Turning on the balls of her bare feet, she grabbed the fishing pole beside the door, jammed a hat on her head and fled, her heart still hammering from his kiss.

THE WORDS ON THE SCREEN blurred and ran together, forming a woman's face.

Pushing away from the computer, Dax ran a hand down his jaw and sighed. Carrie James was the most frustrating woman he had ever met. When she was here, she talked nonstop. Now that she was gone, he still couldn't work. And it was her fault.

All he could think about was the excitement of her small, firm body in his arms, and the toothpaste sweetness of her kiss.

What had come over him? The last thing he wanted was a romantic entanglement. Especially with a woman he didn't especially like.

Resting an elbow on his desk, he cupped his chin in his palm and gazed unhappily around the torture chamber.

The place was so clean it sparkled in the sunlight streaming through polished windows.

Carrie had the softest, most yielding mouth he had ever kissed.

Freshly laundered curtains billowed softly in the breeze off the deck, filling his nostrils with the perfumed scent of tropical blossoms.

The softest, sweetest mouth of any woman he had known.

Yes, they were headed for trouble. He saw this with sudden clarity, as surely as if he had written the tale himself.

This first disturbing kiss would lead to another, then another. In a week or two, dizzy from teasing kisses, they would surrender to the sexual tension fizzing between them, a tension that was becoming almost tangible.

They would go to bed together.

Making love to her would be fantastic. She would be eager and responsive, and he was sure of his own skills in bed. It was the aftermath that gave him pause.

It didn't require a genius to recognize that Carrie James was the type of woman who wouldn't jump into bed with a man unless she had convinced herself that she was in love with him. One had only to glance at the wholesome sprinkle of freckles across the bridge of her nose to grasp that Carrie's standards were formed in stark tones of black and white. Hadn't she dumped Michael What's his name the instant she learned he was married?

If she decided she was in love with Dax to the point of allowing him in her bed, she would want Dax to be in love, too. That was the inevitable next step. That's when the sulking and pouting would start.

He knew exactly how the story would unfold. She would start setting up little tests. She would want him to prove his love by spending every waking minute with her. She would confuse baby talk with love talk and drive him crazy by speaking in a little-girl, wheedling voice. She'd call him Daxy or some other annoying pet name.

Next she would start dropping little hints about weddings and commitment, watching carefully to see if he was receptive. . . .

He shot out of his chair like a bullet. He had to nip this in the bud, right now.

CARRIE LEANED BACK against the rubber rim of the boat and drifted in the cove, the fishing pole at her feet. To her amazement she caught a fish at once and accomplished what she had set out to do. Now she floated aimlessly, enjoying the sunshine and the breeze off the water, reluctant to return to the house.

Dax's unexpected kiss had surprised her. Amazed might be a better description. She had noticed him watching her when he didn't think she knew and had sensed his attraction, but she honestly had not expected him to act on it. Dax Stone was a disciplined man, a man who resisted relinquishing control, plus he didn't especially like or trust her. Yet he had kissed her.

And what a kiss! Carrie tingled and grew red in the face every time she thought about it. That kiss was hotter and more intense than any she had ever experienced. He had held her so fiercely and tightly that she had imagined herself melting into him, fusing with him.

Michael Medlin had never kissed her that intently and powerfully, and she hadn't really wanted him to. She saw now that Michael had been just an interlude, a mistake from the start. Whatever she had felt, it had not been love. Not even close. She had talked herself into that relationship because she was lonely, between boyfriends, and flattered by Michael's pursuit.

The difference between Michael's kiss and Dax's kiss was the difference between a Cub Scout and a Marine. Dax's kiss had rocked Carrie to her toes and left her deeply shaken. Never before had a simple kiss electrified her entire nervous system or made her tremble just to recall it. Never before had a kiss been something more than a kiss, something that reached her on a deep, primal level.

Frowning, she tugged down her hat brim, then crossed her arms over her chest, trying to figure out what had happened.

It was inevitable. The kiss would change things between them in ways she couldn't yet guess. But she knew the sex issue was now on the table. They couldn't ignore their physical attraction any longer, couldn't pretend it didn't exist as they had been doing.

That thought was just a little frightening.

She did not for one minute fear that Dax might force her into something she didn't want or wasn't ready for. But neither did she think he was looking for a lasting relationship. As for her, this was the very worst time to begin a new relationship.

Now where had that thought come from? Puzzled, Carrie searched her mind. Why wouldn't this be the best time to begin a new relationship? Michael was gone, and good riddance. She was footloose and fancy-free, ready and eager to move on with her life.

But there was something . . . what she thought of as The Secret. Something catastrophic that hovered just out of reach, something she fought to bring to the front of her mind, then fled from in panic when it seemed she could almost grasp it.

Bowing her head, Carrie stroked her temples. A war was going on inside of her. One part of her mind urgently demanded to know the secret she was hiding from herself. Another part desperately fought to pretend the secret did not exist.

Occasionally something happened that gave The Secret a surge of power and she could feel it building and bubbling just beneath her awareness, fighting to be known.

Carrie's frown deepened as she thought back over the last hour. There had been the stunning kiss. Her flight to the beach. Thoughts of Michael. Thoughts about Dax.

Was she afraid that Dax would use her and cast her aside as Michael had done? Did The Secret have something to do with that?

Frustration tightened her chest, then she let it go. There was no point upsetting herself by struggling with The Secret. It would surface when she was ready to deal with it or when something happened that shattered her defenses.

What she needed to consider now was Dax and how she felt about him. She had a disturbing suspicion that her heart was following her stirred-up chemistry straight toward him, revving up for engagement. Open for the possibility, at least.

She was primed to make another serious mistake. Carrie had admired Dax's work for years and she was poised to admire the man as well. She respected his level of commitment to his work, thought he was fantastically sexy and handsome, and she liked the way he was willing to meet her halfway about the cleaning and cooking. When he wasn't working, he was polite and mannerly. She didn't confuse his dedication with self-centeredness.

She even saw through the flashes of temper and self-protective defensiveness. He blustered and growled, but she sensed a pussycat lived inside that wide, gorgeous chest.

The sobering truth was, she could fall in love with this man.

But if she did, she would be risking everything, as she had done with no other man. Because Dax Stone believed he didn't need anyone. He was an island unto himself. He didn't want anyone in his life. In less than three months, he would put her on a plane, wave goodbye and carry on as if Carrie James had never invaded his domain.

A woman would have to possess an abundance of foolhardy courage to love a man like Dax Stone. Or be crazy as a June bug.

As if thinking about him had conjured his image, Carrie saw him appear suddenly at the top of the beach, stride into the water, then swim toward her, churning the water with powerful strokes.

Quickly, she grabbed the fishing pole and cast the line toward a gently rolling swell. She didn't want him to think that she was sitting here brooding about his kiss.

His head bobbed up beside the boat, his wet hair sleek and dark, dripping on his shoulders. He hooked his arms over the rubber side and frowned at her.

"We have to talk."

Sunlight sparkled in the water clinging to his lashes. "Talk away," Carrie said, glad she was wearing dark glasses and he couldn't see her eyes. She couldn't tear her gaze from the sensual curve of his lips. "It must be something important to bring you out here."

"I kissed you because I was angry and wanted to shut you up."

"So you said."

"That was the only reason. It didn't mean any-thing and it won't happen again." His stare seemed to penetrate her sunglasses and bore into her. "I don't want you to misunderstand, Carrie. I'm not looking for a relationship."

"I know that. Believe me, neither am I," she said, lifting her chin. "I've had my fill of men, if you want to know. None of you can be trusted."

He rolled his eyes. "This from the woman who can't wait to tell the world where I am and destroy my solitude?" He lifted a hand. "Never mind that. I just want you to know up front that I never intend to marry. There's no future here."

"Excuse me?" She stared at him. "Did someone propose and I missed it?"

"I know how women think. One kiss and all of you start planning the wedding. Well, don't. There's no wedding in my future. Not ever."

"That's a giant leap, isn't it? Jumping from a single kiss to wedding vows? Aside from your stunning arrogance in thinking for one minute that I might want to marry you, why are you so adamant against weddings?" Her voice was tight and angry. He had some nerve. "Have you been married before? A marriage that went sour?"

"I haven't been married and I don't object to weddings. Marriage just isn't for me."

"If you've never been married, then how can you be so sure that you wouldn't like it?"

He stared at her, his dark eyes glittering. "You just don't stop, do you?"

"Enquiring minds want to know," she snapped. They were both angry. "Did your parents have a bad marriage?"

"My parents had a wonderful marriage!"

"Then what's the problem?"

"I'm sterile, damn it!"

For an instant it seemed that time stopped and a pocket of silence dropped over them. When Dax spoke again, shattering the awkwardness, it was as if the bitter words were wrenched from deep in his chest.

"There. Are you happy now? You know something that hasn't appeared in any publication. You have a scoop." If looks could kill, Carrie would have grabbed her heart and keeled over.

"Hold on a second. Let me get this straight. Are you saying that you believe marriage exists solely for the purpose of having children? That unless a couple has children, there's no reason to get married?"

He narrowed his eyes. "Do you know any woman who doesn't want to have children?"

There was something in his gaze, almost a look of pain. Carrie studied his expression carefully, then her eyebrows shot up when she remembered that he came from a large family. She identified the flicker of disappointed yearning in his eyes. "It's you who wants to have children," she said softly, insight dawning and anger evaporating.

"That isn't going to happen," he said flatly, riding the side of the boat as the waves lifted them up and down. Embarrassment darkened his expression as if she had inadvertently stumbled onto his darkest secret. "For whatever reason, I'm not marriage material, that's the point of this discussion."

"Someone hurt you, didn't they?" Carrie said after a minute. She sensed it in a flash, could almost see what had happened. "Someone you cared about, but she wanted children."

Dax directed a glare toward the shore. "Damn it, Carrie, I hate pop analysis. Why do some people think other people welcome instant insights?"

"Was it an instant insight? Am I right?"

"Forget it. What's past is past. What I want you to understand is that I regret kissing you. I don't want you to read something into it that wasn't there. Kissing you was an impulse. There was no deeper meaning." With that, he pushed away from the boat.

"Dax?" she called. He turned his head in the water and looked at her, the sun bronzing the rugged angles of his face. "I liked kissing you."

An involuntary gaze dropped to her lips. "I liked kissing you, too," he admitted after a hesitation, his voice gruff. "That isn't the point." In two strokes he was at the side of the boat. "In less than three months you're going to leave here. And, Carrie, I don't want you climbing on the supply plane thinking you've been used. But if this goes any further, that's what it will be, because it can't be anything else."

She thought for a minute. That's exactly how she would feel if she jumped into bed with a man with whom there could be no possibility of a future. Used. Like Michael had used her.

"You've told me your secret, now I'll tell you mine." The blurted statement astonished her. But it was there. The Secret. Right on the tip of her tongue, demanding to be recognized.

Suddenly Carrie felt like she couldn't breathe, like she was strangling. Panic crushed her like a hot wave and she recoiled from the edge of the boat.

Dax stared up at her, drops of water sliding along his jaw. "Go ahead," he said.

"I...I..."

Dark speckles spun in front of her vision. She started to shake. Despite the hot sun, she felt cold all over.

"I can't," she whispered, the words tumbling over each other. Part of her mind frantically tried to suppress what was coming. But this time The Secret was not going to be denied.

The Secret battered at her mind. It was going to break through and devastate her. She couldn't stop it. She could feel the power building, felt like she was going to explode. And she didn't want to do it in front of Dax.

Dax studied her white face, dropped his gaze to her trembling hands. "Are you all right?"

"I'm fine. I just need a few minutes alone. Please, Dax, just go." He started to protest but she shouted at him. "Go!"

Without a word, he pushed off the boat and swam back to shore.

A whirlwind erupted in her mind. Sterile. Secrets. Michael. Marriage. That last terrible scene on Michael's yacht. Running outside to sit in the very boat she was sitting in now. Sobbing and shocked and devastated and confused and protective.

Because...

Because...

"Oh my God!" Shock widened her eyes.

The air rushed out of Carrie's lungs and a rush of disbelieving tears choked her throat. Trembling and gasping for breath, she wrapped her arms around her body and dropped her head.

"Oh no," she whispered. "Not now. Please, not now." A tremor of rejection and recognition ran through her body. Tears streamed down her cheeks. She couldn't stop shaking. Blindly she lifted her head and tried to see Dax walking across the beach.

"Dax." No sound came out of her lips. "Oh Dax."

Facing the truth changed everything. Now that she knew the secret, her life would never again be the same.

Carrie slid to the bottom of the boat and curled into a ball. She had to face this and accept it. She had no options, none at all. Somehow, someway, she had to accept the truth and find a way to be happy about it.

But how could she?

Chapter Seven

I don't like whiskers on your face or in the sink.
You're not helpless. Clean up after yourself.
                              Maid Marion

Dax stared at the sticky note pasted on the bathroom spigot.

For the past week they had been staying out of each other's way as much as possible. When they had to talk, they spoke with the excessive politeness one reserves for strangers. Carrie seemed distant and distracted. She had taken to communicating through sticky notes.

He found another one on the fridge.

Roses are red
Violets are blue
I don't seem able
to stop interrupting you.
Sorry

P.S. Don't eat the leftovers, they're for supper.

He hated the notes.

And he hated the silence.

And curiosity was nibbling him alive. He kept wondering what secret she had been about to reveal in the boat and why she had changed her mind.

Walking onto the deck, he shaded his eyes and gazed toward the cove where Carrie was bobbing in the water, snorkeling. It was a gorgeous day, hot and clear. Sunlight sparkled on the water, strewing the surface with diamonds. He could see Carrie's hair floating in the water, a strip of red across her back, her neon pink bottom.

Once he pictured her wearing the mismatched bikini, his concentration was blown. The hell with it. He might as well join her. He wasn't going to get any work done today.

Grabbing a mask and snorkel, he strode down to the beach, waved at her and glided into the cool water. Three minutes later he saw her tanned legs through his mask. For all the red top and pink bottom covered, she might as well have been naked.

For a minute or two Carrie ignored him, then she seemed to accept his presence. She touched his arm and pointed to a school of tiny electric blue fish. They were of interest largely because there really wasn't much to observe near the shore. The bottom was sandy, interspersed with feathery growth.

They paddled along the surface, careful not to brush against each other. Dax found himself battling an insane urge to reach over and grab the pink bikini bottom.

When Carrie turned toward the shore, he did, too. She popped her head above water when it was shallow enough for her toes to touch bottom.

"Why do you like snorkeling so much?" he asked, raising his mask. "There isn't much to see."

She tossed her hair back and wiped the water off her face. "This sounds silly, but I keep hoping I'll find a gold doubloon or something wonderful. Wouldn't it be great to be the first person to discover a lost treasure?"

"I suppose." He frowned. "I'm sorry to tell you this, but there's no pirate history attached to this island. It's not likely that you'll find anything valuable."

She bobbed with the motion of the waves, looking at the snorkel she turned in her hands. "Too bad. For once in my life I'd like to do something extraordinary. Something nobody else has done." She gazed toward the horizon. "Life goes by awfully fast. Sometimes you don't get second chances."

The strange tumble of words surprised him. "I'm not following you."

"I know," she said with a sigh. She gazed at him as if she were seeking an answer to some unasked question. "I've been having all kinds of nutty thoughts recently. Thinking about the past . . . and the future."

Sunlight glistened in her wet hair, sparkled like crystal in the droplets hanging on her eyelashes. Her shoulders were tanned to a deep golden color. Dax gazed at her and wondered why women thought they needed makeup. She was beautiful.

"What about the present?" he asked softly. "Are you and I going to continue the silent treatment? And the sticky notes?"

"I don't know that, either."

They stood facing each other, braced against the gentle force of the incoming tide, their bodies swaying with the waves.

She stared deeply into his eyes. "Sometimes you make me really mad."

"Sometimes you make me mad, too." Jumping up in the water, he tossed his mask and snorkel onto the shore. "It's difficult for two people to live together in the best of circumstances. They're bound to rub each other the wrong way on occasion." God. Why did so much of what they said to each other sound like a sexual reference?

Carrie stared at him, then suddenly she lunged at him with surprising strength and pushed his head under water. Dax came up sputtering and gasping, blinking at her in amazement.

He smacked his hand on the surface, spraying her with a jet of water. She yelped, then flung her mask and snorkel toward the beach and lunged at him again. Laughing, he darted to one side, but she dived and caught him by the legs, dragging him under.

When he surfaced, she was wading toward shore. Diving, he stroked forward under water, caught her by the ankles and pulled her into the water. They rolled together, tumbled by the tide, and came up gasping and laughing.

Kicking water at each other, they pulled themselves up the sand and out of the water. Dax tossed her a towel and dried his hair, sneaking peeks as she adjusted the brief bikini.

"What was that all about?" he asked when she was wrapped in the towel and he could look at her directly.

"I don't know, but I feel a little better." She gazed at him for a long moment, then she gathered her mask and snorkel and headed toward the house.

At least they were talking again.

BUT IT STILL WASN'T like it had been. Carrie continued to seem preoccupied. The sticky notes continued.

Dax stared at his computer screen, listening to Carrie doing something in the kitchen. Once again he was not working on his problem novel.

After a while, she walked past him, carrying a broom to the deck. For an instant, Dax stiffened in amazement, thinking she had slapped his shoulder as she passed.

She had, it turned out, but not in anger as he had first supposed. When he touched his shoulder, he discovered she had pasted a sticky note on him. He peeled it off and read it.

You are invited to an evening of food, wine and serious conversation. Drinks and appetizers will be served on the deck at six o'clock.

When he raised his head, Carrie was nowhere to be seen. Only Norman stood in the doorway, watching him with a quizzical expression.

"So what does this mean, Norman, old buddy? First she tries to drown me, then a day later she invites me to dinner."

If Norman knew how to solve the mystery of women, he wasn't telling. Come to think of it, Dax hadn't seen Norman's bossy girlfriend around lately. Maybe parrots suffered relationship problems too.

He scribbled his acceptance on a sticky note and pasted it to the door of the fridge before he went back to work.

A few minutes later, Carrie returned, carrying a cassette player and a box of cassettes. He'd completely forgotten the cassette player in the storeroom.

She placed it near the wicker sofa, then put fresh linens on the bed.

For the next hour or so she worked in the kitchen, creating heavenly aromas fragrant with spices and wine.

Romantic music, fresh bed linens, a gourmet meal... Exactly what kind of evening was Carrie planning?

Dax stared at the computer screen, feeling his stomach tighten. All at once it seemed as if the apricot fragrance of her hair and skin permeated the air around him. His thoughts swam when he realized Carrie was humming a romantic ballad in a throaty register.

He resumed typing, creating nonsense words that he could erase later. All senses alert, he concentrated on Carrie, following her preparations for the evening she was planning.

Resonating with possibilities, he stared blindly at the computer screen for a full hour.

At four-thirty, Carrie left the kitchen and entered the bathroom. A minute later Dax heard the tub filling.

Dazed, he stared into space. There wasn't a doubt in his mind that Carrie was planning a seductive evening. Even after he had warned her that nothing permanent could develop between them.

When no explanation came to mind, he shrugged. He had done the honorable thing. He had told her up front that he was not seeking a lasting relationship. If she was willing to proceed on that basis, well, hell, he was a man, wasn't he? And she was the most desirable woman he'd ever met.

Spirits soaring, suddenly feeling better than he'd felt in weeks, Dax shut off his computer and, after glancing toward the bathroom door, entered the kitchen and peeked into the oven. Next, he examined the wine she had selected, deciding it wasn't quite right for an evening as exciting as this one promised to be. Feverish with anticipation, he hurried out to the storehouse and exchanged Carrie's wine for a Château Brieoux.

When he returned, she was setting the table, humming to a soft tune on the cassette recorder.

The sight of her simply swept Dax's breath away. She had stepped right out of his fantasy. He stood in the doorway, staring, unable to speak.

She wore the green cocktail dress he'd found on the beach. The filmy material floated around her knees when she moved. A sleeveless bodice skimmed the swell of her breasts. Instantly he recalled the green garter belt, but since no stockings had washed ashore, her legs were bare beneath the green hem. With her bare feet and tousled hair, she looked like an exotic Gypsy.

He could not take his eyes off her.

"I didn't use all the hot water," she commented, glancing up from the table. A frown puckered her smooth brow. "You didn't approve of the wine I chose?"

Dax had forgotten the wine bottle dangling in his fingers. "I thought a special dinner deserved a special wine," he said, running a slow, smoldering gaze from her shining hair to the hem of the emerald dress. "You look absolutely spectacular."

On his way to the kitchen, he stopped in front of her and dropped a light kiss on her nose before he put the bottle on the counter, then walked toward the bathroom, popping the snap on his cutoffs and glancing at the clock. He had time to shave again. Whistling happily, he closed the door behind him.

Dumbfounded, Carrie blinked at the bathroom door, listening as the shower came on. Wondering about the kiss on her nose, she opened the wine to let it breathe, checked the table and hors d'oeuvres, hesitated a minute, then approached the bathroom door.

"Dax? Can you hear me?"

He was out of the shower. She could hear water running in the sink. For an instant she felt dizzy, imagining him standing naked in front of the mirror.

"I... Look, don't misunderstand this evening," she called through the door. "I just felt like dressing up, like wearing something besides cutoffs and a tank top. And there's something I need to tell you." She didn't know if he heard her or not. She studied the door a minute, then returned to the kitchen to toss the salad.

When he emerged from the bathroom, she froze, sucked in a quick breath and stared.

Except for the sleek ponytail tied at the back of his neck, this was the Dax Stone she had seen on the television interviews. Elegant and wonderfully big and handsome. Confident, self-sufficient, his male vitality an overwhelming presence.

It seemed to Carrie that the air heated and the room suddenly shrank. Dax filled the house with his presence, large and powerfully virile and masculine. She had believed that he couldn't look more handsome and sexy than he did every day, bare-chested, bare-legged, wearing nothing but the low-slung cutoff jeans that threatened to slide off his hips.

But this was a man born for formal wear, for crisp shirts and tailored jackets, a man who could look casual and elegant at the same instant. He wore a silk tie tonight, a subdued navy and maroon that looked wonderful next to his navy jacket. The white collar against deeply tanned skin made his throat and face look bronzed. This was a drop-dead, fabulous-looking man.

Carrie swallowed hard, suddenly feeling anxious. She knew she had made a serious mistake. This *evening* was a mistake.

Heat rushed into her cheeks, and she bit her lip, frantically trying to think of a way out of the mess that was about to happen.

"What would you like to drink?" she asked in a small voice, her mind racing. There had to be a tactful way to squelch his obvious expectations. That's what she wanted, wasn't it?

"Let me," he said smoothly, passing her on the way to the kitchen. She inhaled a whiff of an expensive after-shave, felt an electric tingle as he lightly touched her arm. "I make a mean daiquiri. Interested?"

Carrie nodded automatically. Sliding onto a stool, she tasted one of the toasted cheese fingers and listened to the bland music she had put on the cassette recorder to fill any awkward silences. A nervous frown creased her brow.

"Ah ... did you hear anything I said to you while you were in the bathroom?"

A relaxed smile curved his lips as he measured rum into the blender. "What did you say?"

"Oh, God." Carrie caught her lip between her teeth and gazed out at a bloodred sunset. She drew a deep breath. "I think I may have given you the wrong idea about tonight."

He slid an iced daiquiri across the counter and sampled a cheese finger. Carrie looked at the drink, but didn't touch it.

"These cheese things are wonderful."

"Look." Carrie drew another breath. "I want to talk to you about something serious, and I thought it would be easier if we did something out of the ordinary like dress up and pretend we were out to dinner."

His drink halted midway to his lips. "Excuse me?"

"I did an article once about how clothing affects behavior, and—" She waved a hand. "Never mind. I suspect you think I'm trying to seduce you or something." Hot color pulsed in her cheeks. "I didn't mean to mislead you, Dax, but seduction isn't the purpose of this evening. I just want to talk."

He lowered his glass to the counter and stared pointedly at her cocktail dress. "We dressed up to talk?"

"I know, it sounds dumb, but I thought..."

"You did all this—" he waved a hand to indicate the hors d'oeuvres and the pork roast "—just so we could talk?"

Carrie's mouth tightened as she watched his expression darken. "I'm sorry I gave you the wrong idea."

Without another word, Dax carried his drink past her and walked onto the deck. Leaning his elbows on the railing, he stared toward the fading sunset, watching the first stars appear and muttering beneath his breath.

Carrie joined him at the railing. "You're angry, aren't you? You thought—"

"Of course I did!"

Her chin rose defensively. "Come on, Dax. I'm not a masochist. You made it very clear that you aren't interested in me. You said we would have no further physical contact. That was *your* rule."

He looked at her through narrowed eyes. "I never said I wasn't interested in you. I said I wasn't the marrying kind"

"You also said you regretted kissing me and it wouldn't happen again."

"Because I assumed you wouldn't want to start something that had no future."

"I don't," she answered, frowning. Somehow when Carrie stood this close to him, her decisions went mushy. She wasn't sure anymore what she thought.

"So what kind of message did you think you were sending when you decided to show up looking like that?" A moody glance swept the material hugging her body. "Or when you changed the sheets and put on romantic music?"

"That isn't romantic music," Carrie protested. "That's elevator music. As for changing the sheets, I did that as a consideration to you!" When she realized how that sounded, color flooded her cheeks and she made a flustered motion with her hands. "Come back inside. Dinner's ready."

Silently he followed her to the table, discarding his tie and jacket along the way. Carrie wished she had an apron to cover the emerald dress and her low neckline. What on earth had she been thinking of?

Neither of them spoke while she carved the roast and arranged the meat and potatoes on a heated platter. "I hope you like candied carrots," she murmured, sitting down and placing a napkin over her lap.

He didn't say anything.

"All right, Dax. I'm sorry. I screwed up. This wasn't a good idea." Dots of color blossomed on Carrie's cheeks. "I should have spelled it out up front. I—"

"Just say whatever it is you wanted to say, okay?" He examined the bottle of Château Brieoux, pressed his lips together in a grimace, then filled their glasses.

"Look, before we leave this... I'm flattered that you were willing to go along with a romantic evening," she said after a minute, her cheeks flaming. Now that she understood how he had interpreted her dress and the dinner, Carrie could hardly think of anything else. Her eyes continually strayed toward the bed, imagining what he had been imagining. Such thoughts made her feel overly warm and tingly all over.

"Flattered? Don't be." Anger washed the gold flecks from his eyes, leaving them almost black. "It's been months since I've had a roll in the hay. I assumed the same applied to you. But that's not true, is it? I forgot about Michael."

Shock froze Carrie's features. She lowered her fork.

"That's a cruel thing to say," she whispered. "First to suggest that if we went to bed together it would only be a roll in the hay, like scratching an itch. And second, to throw Michael in my face. Yes, I went to bed with him," she said, staring into Dax's eyes. Crimson flared on her cheeks. "I thought I was in love with him."

"But you weren't, were you?"

"No, I wasn't." Her voice was as hard and clipped as his. "Michael was a mistake, and I'll be paying for that mistake for the rest of my life!"

They stared angrily at each other across the flowers in the center of the table.

Dax leaned back in his chair and pushed a hand through his hair. "Look, I'm sorry," he said finally. "You're right. I was out of line. When I saw you changing the sheets...I guess I thought—"

"I was only preparing the bed for you." In a different circumstance, the misunderstanding might have been humorous. But not tonight, not with Dax. "I meant what I said about us taking turns in the hammock. Tonight starts my week outside."

"Come on, Carrie. We've settled this. Keep the bed. I don't mind sleeping in the hammock."

"I mind," she said emphatically. "We're going to be fair. We're going to share everything."

His brows raised. "Everything?" he asked. "Why do I get the feeling it's more than just the bed?"

"Yes, there's more. The—the chores." She leaned forward in her chair, her voice growing stronger as she continued. "From now on we're going to share the chores—cooking and cleaning. I'll make up a schedule so we'll know whose turn it is."

Dax threw up his hands. "I don't believe you. You'd make a hell of a master sergeant!"

"Damn right, I would."

He'd lost his appetite. Placing his hands on either side of his plate, he prepared to rise. "If there's nothing else," he said in a cold voice.

"There is." Biting her lower lip and wringing her hands, Carrie stared at her plate. "Remember when I mentioned that thing about having a secret?"

He eased back into his chair. "Yes?"

Carrie turned her head and gazed out the open door. "This is so difficult," she said haltingly. "But I...it's just that you're always praising me for being honest...."

"Go on," he said when she fell silent.

"Well, I haven't been entirely honest with you. Or with myself." She looked at her hands twisting in her lap. "It's only lately that I've been able to face this...and... Well... Oh, God, this is hard!"

"It wasn't easy telling you that I'm sterile," Dax said quietly. "You're starting to worry me. Carrie, something's been bothering you for a while now. We've become friends, haven't we? What could be so bad that you can't tell me?"

"You just don't know!" she said. Crimson flared in her cheeks. "My whole life is a mess because of this!"

Dax's mind raced. What had happened in the last couple of weeks that she would view so drastically? Things had started to change after he kissed her and revealed he was sterile. That day had made them both aware of the sexual tension smoldering between them. Would something like that mess up a woman's life?

"Carrie? What is it? What is the secret you want to tell me?"

"It's... I'm..." She stared at him. "I hate the way you brush your teeth!"

"What?"

She threw down her napkin and ran into the bathroom, the green hem flaring around her knees. She slammed the door behind her.

Bewildered, Dax listened to her deep sobs. He inspected the lovely untouched dinner she had prepared. She had been nervous enough to go to all this work to prepare him to hear... that she hated the way he brushed his teeth?

Unconsciously, he ran a finger over his front teeth, listening to her uncontrollable sobs.

He didn't think so. This was about something else.

Chapter Eight

"Okay, I give up. The hammock is yours. You can have your bed back in six weeks when I leave." She was tired of fighting and losing every night. Sighing, she looked down at another frozen lasagna TV dinner.

After a week of battle waged through sticky notes and rolling eyes, winning this skirmish filled Dax with an absurd burst of pleasure.

The TV dinner was another story. He poked a limp noodle. "Too much for you, huh?"

Carrie tilted her head and shot him a look across the counter. "You could cook a real meal when it's your turn, you know."

"I never learned how." Knowing she watched, he put the containers in the wastebasket, the utensils in the dishwasher and wiped off the countertop. "Do you want some coffee? That I can make."

"About half a cup." When he looked at her in surprise, she shrugged and smothered a yawn. "I'm tired tonight. I think I'll turn in early."

"You spent all day arranging rocks." For reasons utterly unknown to Dax, Carrie had decided to occupy herself by building a decent path to the store-house and to the spring and grotto. He suspected she was looking for a tactful way to get out of the beach house and away from him.

Leaning his arms on the counter, Dax studied her face in the waning light of approaching evening. They ate early when it was his night to cook. "You really do look beat. Why don't you relax tomorrow? Lay in the hammock and read, or go for a swim? The path isn't important."

"I hate unfinished projects." She yawned again, and the overhead light danced in her curls. "But maybe I'll take your advice and give myself a day off."

"Seriously, Carrie, I meant what I said about your cooking. I don't tell you often enough what a terrific cook you are." Frowning, he gazed into his coffee cup. "It's been years since anyone's cooked for me. I guess I'd forgotten how great good food can taste."

"I thought you said you lived with someone for a while. Didn't she cook for you?"

"Laura? Her idea of food was something you ordered in or ate out."

Carried laughed, and her green eyes flickered with curiosity, catching the light. "Tell me about her."

Dax hesitated, not sure he wanted to pursue this line. Finally he shrugged and raised a hand. "I met Laura during a research trip. She'd been to Cannes for the film festival and was in Paris for a week of shopping before she returned to Manhattan. It was the first visit to Paris for both of us. I think we mistook falling in love with the city for falling in love with each other."

Carrie leaned her chin in her palm and gazed at him. "The romance didn't survive the return to reality?"

Frowning, Dax turned his head toward the window. "Laura wanted a baby. I couldn't give her one. End of story."

"I see," Carrie said quietly. Sympathy and understanding softened her expression. Dax studied her for a minute, not liking what he saw. The thought of someone feeling sorry for him was appalling.

To put the moment swiftly behind him, he continued talking. "Laura wasn't in the least domestic. She couldn't cook and wasn't interested in learning. She had no special aptitude for homemaking other than knowing the best decorator and where to hire an efficient maid. But she wanted children."

"You could have adopted."

His mouth pulled down at the corners. "I'm not interested in raising someone else's children. I don't care what anyone says, I can't imagine a real connection or a genuine love for a child that isn't your own."

Carrie turned her face aside, looking out the window. Her voice sounded oddly soft when she said, "I'm sorry the relationship didn't work out."

Surprised, he peered at her. "Don't be. Laura and I weren't right for each other. We would have made each other miserable."

Without thinking about what he was doing, he took her hand and examined it. Carrie's hands were small and square, the nails short and unpolished. It occurred to Dax that if he was writing about her, he would describe her hands as capable and expressive, hands that could bake a pie or build a path, hands that spoke when she did, gesturing to emphasize, underscore or explain.

"I'm glad you don't wear nail polish," he said.

"I do sometimes," she said in an odd-sounding voice.

Suddenly he realized he was caressing her hand. Awareness shot through his body like a jolt of adrenaline. Her hand was soft yet firm, her skin warm against his. He inhaled the sunshiny apricot fragrance of her, felt the nearness of her long legs next to his. When he turned his head, he gazed into luminous green eyes that seemed to capture the fading light and glow from within.

During the time they gazed deeply into each other's eyes, worlds collided. New stars were born. One era passed and another began. When Carrie withdrew her hand from his, Dax blinked as if emerging from a trance.

"I think I'll take a warm bath and call it an early night." Her cheeks were flushed and her mouth trembled at the corners. She backed away from the counter, then turned and hurried toward the bathroom door.

Dax stared after her. What the hell had happened just now? Standing on shaky legs, he walked around the counter, opened the fridge and took out a cold beer. Closing his eyes, he rolled the icy bottle across his forehead.

After a minute he heard water running in the bathroom, filling the tub. He could imagine her naked, surrounded by perfumed bubbles as vividly as if he was standing beside the tub gazing down at the damp tendrils curling around her cheeks.

Swearing softly, he gripped the beer bottle so tightly that his knuckles turned white. The sound of splashing water ceased. He imagined her leaning back, perhaps lifting one sleek leg to inspect the curve.

Grinding his teeth together, Dax put the beer bottle in the sink, grabbed his jogging shoes, then walked out the door and down to the beach.

He ran along the hard-packed sand, pushing himself through the starry darkness until his breath seared his lungs and his muscles twitched and burned. Dropping forward, he kicked off his shoes, then placed his hands on his knees and gasped for air, letting the night waves swirl around his ankles.

What was happening to him? All he could think about was sex and Carrie. Carrie and sex. He couldn't sleep at night, was aware every time she turned in bed or sighed in her sleep. He couldn't keep his mind focused on his work for thinking about her, wondering what she was doing, where she was. Every time he looked at her, he saw silky firm flesh and the glow of healthy vitality. He could lose himself in the depths of her green, green eyes. Could waste an hour staring at his computer screen thinking about the sparkle of her smile or recalling the sound of her laughter.

This small, lush woman had come into his calm, solitary life and had spun his world into a whirlwind chaos. He couldn't work, couldn't sleep and couldn't concentrate. His thoughts followed her like iron drawn to a magnet. She annoyed him, frustrated him, fascinated him and kept him in a nearly constant state of arousal.

"Damn it to hell!" He brought a fist down hard on his knee.

He did not want this kind of distraction, did not need a woman in his life. He didn't need anyone. In particular he did not want or need Carrie James.

Except he desired her like he had desired no other woman in his life.

Straightening, he wiped the sweat from his face and throat, then tilted his head to stare at a black canopy that glowed with the fire of distant stars.

Damn it. Why couldn't the supply plane come tomorrow?

READING DIDN'T RELAX Carrie as she had hoped it would. The hammock was comfortable, that wasn't the problem. The problem was she had only to lift her eyes from the page and she was looking through the door and into the house at Dax's strong profile.

Once she discovered that, she lost all interest in the book she was trying to read. The only thing she could think about was Dax.

If she was honest with herself, she had to admit that Dax had been the primary focus of her thoughts for several weeks. He was the center of her days and the reason she tossed and turned at night.

Releasing a long, deep breath, she adjusted her sunglasses on her nose, then looked through the door.

He sat wide-legged in front of his computer, glaring at the screen as if he hated it. Knots rose along his jawline. The muscles swelled on his shoulders, then he leaned forward and moved his fingers across the keyboard, hesitated, then swore between his teeth. His wrists went limp and he tilted his head back, exposing a long, corded expanse of throat.

Carrie dropped her head and made herself look down at the book shaking in her hands. She wet her lips and swallowed.

Everything Dax Stone did carried a sexual charge. Even sitting in front of his computer, he reminded her of a jungle animal bursting with virility and power. It wasn't anything he consciously did. Dax's sexuality was an integral part of him, as natural to him as the way he walked or the way he looked into the eyes of the person he was talking to. Carrie doubted he was aware that he threw off masculine sparks as exciting as a fireworks display. She doubted he ever considered how his cutoffs moved on his hips when he walked or what his tanned body looked like in the sun.

Closing her eyes, she recalled the firm, well-defined contour of his lips, remembered the moment when he had kissed her. The memory quickened her breathing and brought a sheen of moisture to her forehead. She would never forget that kiss and her electric response. No man had ever made her feel like she had felt in Dax's arms.

The moment when his lips claimed hers, Carrie had felt more alive than at any other time in her life. She'd felt the blood rushing through her body, had heard her pulse singing in her ears. Her body had turned liquid and melted into his. And it had felt so right, so perfectly right, like two pieces of a jigsaw puzzle coming together.

Stretching in the hammock, she was suddenly aware of the coarse canvas against her bare midsection and the backs of her legs, aware of the warm air sultry with the heavy, perfumed scent of tropical blossoms. Aware of the heat and the heaviness of her body. Aware that

Dax was only a few feet away. The bed was only a few feet away.

A despairing groan wrenched from her chest.

"Mmm?" Dax called from inside. "Did you say something?"

His deep voice resonated inside her. Carrie closed the book on her stomach and clenched her fists on top of it. She had to get out of here, away from the sight of his bare chest and heavy legs. Away from the curl of hair tied in a ponytail at the back of his neck, that curl that she longed to touch in the worst way.

"I... I'm going to find something different to read, then go to the grotto," she called, looking at the hot sky through the leaves of a feathery palm. It would be cooler there, balm for heated thoughts.

"Mmm. Sounds like a good idea."

His absent tone made her smile. When Dax was working, she wasn't sure he realized what he was saying or was even aware that he spoke at all. For all his complaining about interruptions, Carrie would have wagered all she owned that he didn't notice half of them.

Inside Carrie found a beach towel, stared for a long moment at the deep ridge running down Dax's bare back, then she slipped from the door and almost ran up the path to the spring and grotto.

As she had hoped, it was cooler in the grotto, and so lovely that an ache opened inside her chest.

Clear, fresh spring water trickled over a spoon-shaped rock, splashing into a small, inviting pool. Lacy ferns draped the rim of the pool, interspersed with wild orchids and fragrant clusters of yellow thunbergia. The strong, sweet scent of creamy frangipani perfumed the air.

On an impulse, Carrie picked one of the delicate wild orchids and tucked it behind her ear. Then, smiling at a fanciful image of nymphs cavorting in a sylvan glade, she hesitated not a second before she stripped off her clothes and stretched out on the beach towel in a patch of filtered sunlight.

Nude sunbathing was something she hadn't done since college and hadn't really expected to ever do again. But the primal perfection of the grotto seemed to demand a return to nature. And the air and light on her body felt wonderful.

Besides, she was utterly assured of privacy. Dax was totally absorbed in his work. Very likely he thought she was still reading in the hammock and didn't realize she had gone.

Wearing nothing but her sunglasses and a smile, Carrie stretched languidly on the towel, then focused her full concentration on the book she had brought to read.

DAX DIDN'T understand it. For a while the words had poured out of him like a swiftly moving stream. Then, almost like turning off a tap, he went dry. Frowning in frustration, he pushed back from the computer and ran a hand over his face.

This ought to be an ideal moment for unfettered creation. Carrie was gone, and even Norman and his pals were unusually quiet today.

So why was he unable to concentrate?

Annoyed, Dax went into the kitchen, looking for a box of instant soup. Maybe he was hungry.

He ate the soup sitting on the counter, trying to recall where Carrie had gone. He vaguely remembered her telling him that she was going somewhere.

He stared at the soup for a moment, then made a face and set it aside. He knew what he was hungry for, and it wasn't soup.

Carrie was driving him crazy. He could not get her out of his mind. Everywhere he looked, he saw her.

She influenced everything he thought and did. His Great American Novel sizzled with sex scenes. Steam practically wafted off the pages. He didn't know how that had happened. Certainly he had not intended to write a sexy novel.

And he hadn't planned on Carrie. Not once had he imagined his solitary escape would be interrupted by the appearance of the most desirable woman ever created. And that's how he saw her.

"Damn it."

Dropping his head, he pressed his fingertips against the frown line creasing his brow.

Maybe if he talked to her about it.... Sometimes bringing problems into the open diminished their impact and robbed them of the power to distract. He thought about that.

Carrie was the easiest person to talk to he'd ever met. Surely they were sophisticated enough to have a frank discussion about sexual attraction and how to cope with it. As for getting into the subject . . . words were his business. He'd think of a tactful opening.

Sliding off the counter, Dax shook his hair loose from the ponytail, gave a determined nod, then walked out the door. He'd try the beach first, then the grotto.

THE MOMENT Dax stepped into the cool, filtered shade of the grotto and looked toward the pool, he was lost. Everything he had planned to say dropped out of his mind like falling rocks. His mouth dried and his body went rigid.

She was naked. Gloriously and magnificently naked. Gold and sun-bronzed and rose-tipped naked.

Carrie floated in the pool, her arms spread and her eyes closed, her face lifted to a patch of sunshine. Her hair waved around her small head like a dark halo, broken only by the creamy glow of the orchid tucked beside her temple.

Petals from the frangipani tree drifted on the surface of the pool, surrounding her lush, perfect body. Dax felt as if he had stumbled into a myth, intruded on a bathing goddess.

Crystalline water caressed the sides of full, pink-tipped breasts, flowed over her waist to pool above her stomach and below, where her legs met in a sweet, dark triangle.

He stared at her in helpless awe and understood that she was every man's dream, every man's fantasy, a vision so erotically perfect that the sight of her stopped his heart. She was Diana and Athena and the Lady of the Lake. She was Sleeping Beauty awaiting a man's awakening. She was a nymph caught in a moment of dreaming, a fairy creature too achingly lovely to exist in reality.

If she hadn't opened her eyes and seen him, Dax might have quietly withdrawn, too moved by the sight of her golden beauty to intrude on her solitude, too aroused to call attention to himself without embarrassment.

It didn't surprise Carrie to open her eyes and discover Dax standing at the edge of the pool gazing at her. Her thoughts must have conjured him into her dream. Languid and half intoxicated by the sylvan beauty of the grotto, she floated in a perfumed mirage somewhere between fantasy and reality.

In this fantasy Dax would find her. And when he appeared, he would look exactly as he did now, standing tall on the rocks above her, his hair freed of the ponytail, swirling wild around his face and shoulders. Sunlight and shadow bronzed his chest and the muscles rising on his thighs. His eyes were dark and intense, his gaze narrowed and aflame with desire as he stared at the gentle lap of water pooling between her legs.

Time shimmered and slipped. In this moment they were no longer Carrie and Dax. They were Woman and Man, alone in a lush, verdant Eden steaming with primal heat and the musky scent of moss and earth beneath the sweetness of perfumed blossoms.

Breath quickening, her heart pounding, Carrie lifted her arms out of the water, the gesture an embrace and an invitation.

Eyes holding hers in a smoldering stare, Dax jerked open the snap on his cutoffs and tore down the zipper. The cutoffs slid down his muscled thighs, and he stood above her naked in the green-filtered sunlight. Rampant, powerful, a god rising out of rock and foliage. Muscle and sinew tightened into bronzed magnificence. At this moment, he was primal, mythical.

For an instant neither of them moved. They looked at one another, breaths coming faster, hearts pounding, the stealing weakness of desire thrusting against the mounting heat of passion.

Then Dax's arms raised above his head, drawing his stomach taut and flat, and he dived into the pool, slicing into the water so cleanly that he left only a ripple in his wake.

He surfaced beside her, his sleek, wet head emerging at her waist. Unable to speak, warm breath panting from parted lips, Carrie gazed at him as his feet found the bottom of the pool and he rose above her, the movement scattering the petals floating on the surface.

"You are so beautiful," he murmured in a hoarse whisper. "So magical and lovely."

Bending, he cupped her head in one hand and kissed her, supporting her floating body with his other arm. Drops from his hair fell on Carrie's breast, the coolness contrasting with the searing heat of his lips. He kissed her deeply, totally, taking her mouth as if the secret of life could be found within, in mingling tongues, in each other's taste and touch.

When he released her lips, leaving her gasping and breathless, hot kisses followed the arch of her throat to the full swell of her breasts. He licked the droplets of water from her hard nipples and from beneath her breasts. And where his lips touched her skin, a flame ignited and ran like a fiery arrow to the very center of her desire.

If he had not continued to support her, Carrie believed she would have sunk beneath the water. Her body felt heavy and swollen with the burning weight of passion. Her eyelids dropped and her lips parted.

And she moaned softly as his hand stroked her breasts, cupped her stomach, then slipped between her legs, caressing, stroking, exploring, teasing them both to gasping heights of urgency.

"Dax!" The word emerged like a whispered explosion, a plea. She couldn't breathe, couldn't think of anything except the heat he was teasing from her body.

He turned her in his arms, catching her by the waist as she sank, his mouth coming down hard to plunder and ravage hers.

The world spun above them as their naked bodies met beneath the petal-strewn surface. Carrie felt the coolness of the water close around her legs and buttocks, felt the fiery heat of Dax's thighs and glistening torso.

"Dax . . ." The single word was a sob of need and longing.

When he lifted her, then entered her it was like a rod of fire piercing the coolness around her. She wrapped her legs around his upper thighs and gripped his shoulders, feeling his hands on her waist, moving her, controlling her, guiding the tempo of a pagan coupling that rocked them both into breathless, mindless passion.

Carrie felt herself soaring, a Roman candle illuminating the grotto with an explosion of heat and fire, a shining flash of emotion and stunning sensation. And then she was contracting inward, blindly pulling him deeper, deeper into her very center.

When the fire storm ended, she fell limp against Dax's chest, gasping for breath, her body trembling violently beneath his stroking hands. She heard his breath fast and harsh in her ear, felt his heart racing beneath her cheek.

After several minutes, Dax lifted her face from his chest and kissed her gently, lingeringly.

"I have never in my life experienced anything remotely like that," he said in a thick voice, gazing deeply into her eyes. "I will never forget this, Carrie. Not ever."

"Did you...?" Suddenly she felt guilty. She had tried to think of Dax and his pleasure, but what he was doing to her had shot mind and flesh into a realm of pure, selfish sensation. She hadn't been able to think, only to feel and react with an intensity more powerful than anything she had ever experienced.

He laughed and grinned at her. "Yes. I did."

They stood together in the pool, holding each other by the waist, gazing into each other's eyes.

"I think I knew you would come here," Carrie said softly. "Not at first, but after I entered the pool. It just seemed...inevitable. Like a dream that was fated to happen."

"I came to talk to you about sex," he said, smiling.

"I'm in favor of it." She kissed his chin and returned his smile.

"Carrie..." But he changed his mind about whatever he had been about to say. Instead, he wrapped his arms around her and held her close, resting his chin on her wet head.

"This is going to change things," Carrie murmured after a minute. "And that frightens me a little. What happens next, Dax?"

"Next?" Easing back, he smiled at her. "We get out of this pool, dry off and maybe take a nap in the sun."

"That sounds wonderful." He hadn't answered the question she had actually asked, but Carrie could accept that perhaps it was too soon for questions. They both had some thinking to do.

Dax climbed the rocks rimming the pool, turned and extended a hand to help her. When she stood before him in the grotto's watery, otherworldly light, Dax let his gaze travel slowly over the lushly rounded curves of her body.

"You look like a water nymph. You're truly the loveliest woman I've ever seen." A glow of renewed desire kindled in his dark gaze. "Did you bring a towel?" he asked in a gruff voice. "I'll dry you."

Carrie's lips curved in a sensual smile. "The towel's behind you."

And so was the book she had brought to the grotto.

For an instant her heart stopped in her chest. She froze and her eyes widened.

"Dax, wait." Stepping forward, she reached for his arm.

But she was too late. Dax stopped mid-stride and stared in shock at the manuscript pages laying beside her clothing. Stunned, he knelt and read a few lines as if he couldn't believe this manuscript could be his, as if perhaps there were another novelist on the island.

He stood and turned, his face dark with fury.

Chapter Nine

"How dare you do this!"

Carrie cringed at the accusation and rage blazing in Dax's expression. His fists were clenched, and furious emotion burned in his eyes. Suddenly feeling vulnerable and exposed, she grabbed the towel and clutched it in front of her nakedness.

Her head dropped, and she touched a shaking hand to her forehead. Then her chin came up and she met his eyes. She gripped the towel so tightly that she could feel her fingernails biting into her palms through the material.

"I was curious about what you're working on, so I just . . . I took one of the drafts to read."

"Damn it!" Swearing furiously, he bent for his cutoffs and jerked them on with hard, angry movements. "I've told you a dozen times that my work is off limits. I told you that no one—*no one*—reads my work until it's finished!"

"Dax, I'm sorry. I apologize. I had a crazy idea that maybe I could help if I knew what you were working on. And I . . . I wanted to be the first person to read it. I just—"

"I should have known I couldn't trust you." Grinding his teeth, he slapped his forehead. "What in the hell was I thinking about? I've known from the first minute that you plan to sell me out the instant you can. Yet I left a half dozen drafts lying around in plain sight. I didn't even make it difficult for you. No, like the world's worst idiot, I asked you to respect my privacy and professional integrity and trusted that you would." Bitterness and fury burned in his stare. "That's a laugh, isn't it? I trusted you!"

Carrie felt the blood drain from her face. Her fingers shook and she felt cold. "I don't know what to say," she whispered.

"Don't say anything! I mean it, Carrie. Not one word!"

So angry that he was trembling, Dax bent and scooped up the manuscript pages, jumbling them together. Without looking at her, he turned and strode rapidly down the path. In a moment the encroaching foliage swallowed him, and there was no sound in the grotto except the silver splash of falling water and the sick pounding of Carrie's heart.

Still clutching the towel, she sank to her knees on the mossy earth beside the pool, trying to catch her breath.

Confusion blinded her. One moment she had been soaring on wings of rapturous sensation, radiant in the steamy light glowing from Dax's dark eyes. The next moment she had crashed to earth in pain and embarrassment.

Carrie tucked her knees under her and curled in on herself, covering her face with the towel. A tremor of guilt and anguish rocked her body.

She shouldn't have taken the manuscript. There was no excuse for what she had done. She knew how Dax felt, knew how protective he was of his work.

The temptation had simply been too great. For years Dax Stone had been her favorite author. Of course she wanted to read his latest work. And she really had cherished a tiny hope that she might be able to offer helpful suggestions. It was no secret that this book tormented him.

Releasing the towel, she raised her hands and pressed the heels of her palms against the moisture swimming in her eyes.

Dax thought he was a fool because he had trusted her.

That knowledge cut through her like a hot knife. And the blade twisted painfully when she recalled how moments before they had held each other in ecstasy. They had shared something extraordinary that most people never experienced in a lifetime.

Now Dax believed that she had betrayed him.

And she had. There was no way around the truth.

Dropping her face into her hands, Carrie wept until she felt weak and drained.

The worst of it was that she knew now that she loved him. Her foolish heart had settled on a hopeless cause. She loved a man who thought his strength resided in needing no one, a man who didn't recognize his deep loneliness or admit to it. She loved a man who had chosen a solitary life and protected his choice like a threatened tiger. She loved a man who had briefly desired her but who saw her as an annoyance and an intrusion, as a menace ready to betray him at the earliest moment.

If there had been any way off the island, any way at all, Carrie would gladly have seized the opportunity to flee. She would rather have swum through shark-infested waters than walk to the house and face Dax.

Moving in slow motion, she dressed, then turned toward the path, wiping tears from her eyes and placing one reluctant foot in front of another.

Black clouds rose ominously in the eastern sky, blanking out the horizon. It seemed fitting.

At the foot of the stairs leading to the deck Carrie paused and listened to the slamming and banging coming from the house.

Her courage failed. Continuing along the path, she hurried to the beach, looked around a minute, then spotted the rubber boat she had arrived in. Dax had dragged it up the beach to a shady spot near where the explosive undergrowth rimmed the sand.

After climbing inside the boat, she pulled her bare knees up under the oversize man's shirt she wore, wrapped her arms around her legs and focused sad eyes on the horizon.

A storm was moving in fast. The humid air thickened and felt heavy and damp on her skin. Beyond the cove the sea tossed and reared. Carrie had come to the water seeking comfort, but nature's growing turbulence reflected the turmoil in her heart. She lowered her forehead to her raised knees and closed her eyes.

The part of her that seemed so attuned to Dax sensed his presence a full minute before she watched him burst out of the foliage edging the path and stride across the beach toward the water. Lifting her chin, Carrie noticed the dark clouds boiling directly overhead and wondered how long she had been sitting hunched in the rubber boat.

"Carrie!" His shout roared into the spray blowing inland.

She didn't want to face him. She felt bad enough without further castigation. But there was no place to hide.

"Up here," she called finally, "in the boat."

The rising wind tossed her words away, and Dax didn't hear. She had a moment to observe the big, clean lines of his magnificent body. Even wearing nothing but his cutoffs, he carried himself like a young prince, like he owned the universe. Head high, his loose hair blowing in the strengthening breeze off the water, he peered along the curve of the cove.

She also noticed that his fists were clenched at his sides. He was in control, but he was still furious.

Carrie cleared her throat, dreading the coming confrontation, and called to him again. This time he heard and strode rapidly up the sand. He stopped in front of the boat and stared at her with hard, cold eyes.

"Dax, I really am sorry—"

He made a chopping motion with one hand, brushing aside her apology. "I have to know," he said in a harsh voice. "What did you think of the book?"

The question shouldn't have surprised her— She was a writer, too, and understood the vulnerability involved in showing someone her work. But it had never occurred to her that a writer of Dax Stone's stature might share the same insecurities.

"I didn't have time to read the complete manuscript," she said after a minute, gazing up at him.

Lightning split the sky behind him. For an instant Dax loomed as a majestic silhouette against a blinding white sky. Carrie saw the dark outline of his tossing hair, his bare shoulders swelling with tension and anger.

When her vision cleared, he was staring at her, his dark eyes as hard as iron. Waiting.

"It's not... Well, I thought..." Carrie hedged, stalling. God, she hated this. In some ways this moment was worse than the scene at the grotto.

Dax didn't speak a word. He stood planted on the sand, fists clenched on his hips, staring at her with accusation and expectation.

Carrie bit her lips and drew a deep, shaky breath. Then she steeled herself, lifted her head and gazed into the anger burning in his eyes.

"The book stinks."

DAX STOOD RIGID and deadly silent, continuing to stare at her. A crack of lightning made her jump. Turning abruptly, Dax faced away from her, scowling at the frothy chop that had appeared on the waves.

"It isn't a Dax Stone book," Carrie tried to explain, focusing on the tense muscles rising in sharp definition along his back. "When I read a book of yours, I expect to be scared out of my wits."

His muscles twitched, but he didn't speak.

"I know you want the reviewers to take you seriously, and maybe a literary novel will force them to look at you differently," she said, speaking to his back. "But, Dax, who are you writing for? A handful of snotty reviewers—or a million readers who love your scary books?"

He turned to her and kicked the sand. "Damn it, you don't know what you're talking about. It's time to grow, to create something new!" He threw out his hands. "I can't write the same old stuff anymore." His head fell back, and he glared at the low black cloud ceiling. Knots pebbled his jaw. "Hell, I can hardly write at all! You've seen the struggle. The sentences have no life, no creative force. There's no zest or energy to the work anymore. Can you understand that?"

Carrie sat in the boat like a lump of stone, her heart beating painfully in her chest. She hated saying these things to him, knowing each of her words fell like a blow. As furious as he was that she had read his manuscript, he still wanted to hear her say the work was wonderful. With all her heart Carrie wished she could have lied and told him what he wanted to hear.

But lying wasn't in her character. Neither was doing things halfway.

So upset and tense that she didn't notice the first fat raindrops strike the rim of the boat, Carrie drew a long, reluctant breath and looked at him. Her arms around her legs were rigid.

"The problem with your work isn't about writing, Dax. It's about you."

He whirled in the sand and faced her angrily. "What the hell is that supposed to mean?"

"You're a fraud."

"*What?*"

"You're deluding yourself, hiding from the truth." For an instant Carrie pictured the shaggy beard he had worn when she first met him. But when she looked at him now, all she could think about was how much she hated doing this, how much she wished they could end this conversation right now, this minute.

"I think you'd better explain," he said, speaking through his teeth. Fury burned in his dark, intense stare.

"You not only ran away to this island, but you're running away inside, too."

He stepped toward the boat, so angry he was shaking. Carrie pushed to her feet and stepped onto the sand, shoving at the hair that whipped around her cheeks and eyes.

"You'd better damned well be able to back up those statements!"

She dashed a raindrop from her face with a trembling hand. Her heart was beating with painful force against her rib cage. "Listen to yourself. Your sentences have no life, no impact, no creative force. You've gone dry. You can't perform." She drew a halting breath, feeling his fury vibrating around her as tangibly as the powerful wind and rattling palm fronds.

"That's right!" A flare of lightning lit his eyes, almost black with emotion. "I can't perform."

"Oh, Dax, don't you see the correlation? You ran away from life when you learned you were sterile. You turned your back on civilization and told yourself that you didn't need anyone, not a wife, not a family or friends. You couldn't make Laura accept you as you are and you couldn't change the doctor's diagnosis. But you could change your writing. You could make the reviewers accept you. You could leave genre writing behind and give birth to something new."

"That's crazy!"

"Except you see yourself as flawed. You're expressing the trauma of physical sterility in your work, stripping away the creative energy. Don't you see? You're creating the problems with your writing because the shock of learning you were sterile ran so deep that—"

"That is the stupidest, most ridiculous nonsense I ever heard!" His furious shout rose above the din of the building storm. The palms swayed noisily above them, and water hissed on the shore. Rain soaked them, plastering their clothing to their tense bodies.

"Dax, please. Just—"

"Shut up, Carrie. I mean it. What you're saying is utter crap!" A sneer of anger and rejection twisted his lips to one side. "Since when did you get a degree in pop psychology? What makes you think you can read a few pages and go on to psychoanalyze my life?"

Anger rushed through Carrie's body. Stepping forward, she shouted at him, feeling the sting of raindrops pelting her face.

"Don't tell me to shut up, Dax. That isn't acceptable. *You* came down here looking for me. *You* asked my opinion. You have no right to get angry because you don't like the opinion you asked to hear!"

"How calm would you be if I told you how stupid you were to go chasing after a married man?" Even though they stood almost toe-to-toe, they had to shout to be heard over the booming thunder and cracking lightning. The palm fronds rattled like sabers above them. Raindrops hammered against the foliage. "Or that an entire unflattering character analysis could be drawn from your willingness to betray someone who probably saved your life!"

The fight drained out of her. His words stung, but she understood he was lashing out in pain and anger, saying whatever he thought would wound her. And he instinctively found the target. What he said hurt.

Carrie dropped her wet head and covered her eyes with a shaking hand. "Why are we doing this to each other?" she whispered. After stumbling back a step, she lifted eyes brimming with pain and bewilderment. "A few hours ago we were making love... Now we're attacking each other. Oh, Dax."

Turning, slipping in the wet sand, blinded by blowing rain, Carrie ran toward the path, bending against the ferocious wind. A flying twig struck her arm, leaving a red scratch. A jagged bolt of lightning stabbed the tossing sea.

When she reached the steps leading to the dark house, Carrie looked around her with an expression as wild as the storm. No, she couldn't go inside and wait for him. Dax hated her.

Feeling strangled by the tears choking her throat, she turned off the path and plunged blindly into the thick foliage.

DAX THREW BACK his head and roared his outrage into the storm.

It was crazy to suggest that because he couldn't create life with his body he wouldn't allow himself to create life on the page. It was an insulting and offensive example of thumbnail psychology offered by a woman who had betrayed his trust not once but twice.

And then she had the effrontery to tell him that the work he had not given her permission to read was crap, and it was crap because he was sterile. Because he no longer believed in himself. Because he was hiding from the pain and shock of a new, empty vision of Dax Stone.

Shaking with the need to strike out, he kicked the rubber boat, sending it skidding across the wet sand into the dripping foliage. He wanted to rip the shrubs out of the ground with his bare hands, wanted to tear the heavens apart like the lightning that cracked around him.

Jerking his fist back, he struck the trunk of a palm tree bent nearly double by the wind. Pain rocketed up his arm. Clenching his teeth, Dax pulled his bloodied knuckles close to his chest, feeling the rage leave him in a rush that left him feeling dizzy.

What was he doing? Sinking to his knees in the wet sand, he leaned a hand against the palm trunk and braced against the wind. Rain poured down his face and torso in sheets.

He was sterile.

He would never sire a child. Nothing of Dax Stone would live on after he was gone. He would never hold a child of his own next to his heart and dream the dreams of a father. No one would ever call him Dad or slip a small hand into his. He would never know what it was to watch his child grow and move into adulthood, or experience the pride and love and small annoyances of parenthood. He was destined to miss the primary joy of a man's existence.

He could have given so much love to a child.

Pitching forward, Dax covered his face with his hands and wept uncontrollably. Bitter tears of helplessness and loss mixed with the rain stinging his face.

A storm raged in his heart, as wild and ferocious as the storm crashing around him.

He had always believed that some day he would have an adored wife and a houseful of laughing, rambunctious children. But he, whose very identity was embedded in the idea of family, he was sterile. The beloved uncle of his nieces and nephews would never hold a son or a daughter of his own.

A deafening crack of lightning boomed through his anguish, followed by a scorched odor and the sound of splintering wood.

Reacting instinctively, Dax jerked into a ball and rolled out from under the palm seconds before the tree crashed to the sand, shaking the earth beneath his body. Fingers of bright flame flickered on the charred stump before sputtering out in the rain.

Adrenaline flooded his nerves as he jumped to his feet and stared at the fallen tree. He could have been crushed. Or struck by lightning. A long shudder ran down the length of his body.

As if emerging from a lengthy slumber, Dax raised his head and leaned into the wind, surveying the ongoing fury of the storm. Furious waves reared high and tossed foam and spray into the blowing air before hurling up the beach. Small branches and broken leaves swirled in the dark air. A downed tree lay across the path leading to the house.

Carrie! Where was she? Was she all right?

Oh, God. Closing his eyes, Dax swayed, buffeted by the wind. She hadn't insulted him. She'd been honest with him. Carrie was the first person he'd met in a long, long while who had the courage to risk absolute honesty.

And she had forced him to confront a bitter and painful truth that he'd been running from. He had believed he'd come to terms with a childless future, but he hadn't. Maybe he never would. Maybe his grief would endure the rest of his life. But he sensed he would be able to work now. Or soon, anyway.

Carrie's honesty had made that possible. In return, he had attacked her and driven her away. Into the heart of a storm as wild and fierce as the one that had brought her to him.

"Carrie!"

He took off running, leaping over the fallen tree on the path, climbing over a larger specimen that had crashed down across the bottom of the steps leading to the house. He burst into the house and flicked the light switch. Nothing happened, but a flash of lightning showed him that she wasn't there.

Feeling a stab of panic, he climbed the railing and dropped to the ground, then ran to the storehouse. She wasn't there, either.

"Carrie!" He cupped his hands around his mouth and shouted. The wind tossed her name back in his face. "Carrie!"

A leaf-laden branch flew against his chest with enough force to knock Dax to his knees. He fought free of the wet leaves and watched the branch spiral away in the wind.

"Carrie!" Sudden fear thinned his shout. Bending, he shoved aside drenched foliage, praying the pounding rain had not washed away her footprints. He had to find her.

If anything happened to Carrie, he would never forgive himself.

Chapter Ten

Carrie was lost and terrified.

Lightning ripped the sky, one jagged flash following upon another, blinding her, then plunging her into wet blackness. The electric crack of lightning, the rolling growls of thunder and the loud hammering of rain on wide leaves made it impossible to hear the sea and thus get her bearings.

This part of the island was utterly unfamiliar. She hadn't realized the spongy earth gave way to rocky terrain and climbed sharply the farther she moved inland. But lightning revealed the evidence. She had circled to a sheer, vine-draped rock face.

Wiping the rain from her eyes and lashes, Carrie stared at the jutting layers of rock rising high above her. "Not again!"

She was drenched and chilled to the bone, confused and disoriented. As she stood in the wet, waist-high foliage, shivering and frightened, a spear of lightning struck the rock face five feet above her and to her left. Carrie screamed and jumped backward as a shower of mud and leaves and chunks of rock tumbled to the ground a few yards from her sandals.

Wild-eyed and shaking, she wrapped her arms around her body and tried to think what to do.

Somewhere nearby a tree splintered and crashed to the ground, shaking the earth beneath her feet. She was positive the winds had reached gale force, buffeting her one way, then the other. Stinging strands of hair whipped against her cheeks. The rain pounded down in a solid sheet.

"Oh, God." An acrid smell of charred wood pinched her nostrils, telling her that she was not imagining the lightning strikes all around her. What was she going to do? She needed shelter and warmth. She could not believe she had been so stupid as to run into unknown territory in the middle of a raging tropical storm.

Sinking to her knees, she peered into the blackness of drenched foliage, despair thudding in her chest. It all looked the same. Dark, wet and inpenetrable. Only the glistening rock face told her that she'd been here before.

"Carrie!"

Her head jerked up and she strained to hear over the din of the storm. Had she imagined Dax's voice? All she could hear was thunder and the hammering of raindrops.

"Carrie? Carrie!"

Yes! Thank God. Pulling herself out of the mud, she spun in a circle, straining to peer through the wall of rain and night black foliage.

"Here!" she screamed, hearing the fear and hope in her voice. "I'm over here!"

She didn't see Dax until he almost stumbled into her, then she flung herself into his arms, sobbing with relief. His powerful arms closed around her fiercely, crushing her against his body.

"You scared me to death!" he said close to her ear. "Don't ever run off the path again!"

"I got lost and I was so frightened!" Lightning speared the earth close by, shaking the ground and leaving a heavy sizzle of ozone in the air. Carrie's hands flew over his face, his wet bare chest. "Are you all right?" A half dozen scratches had left pink marks on his chest and shoulders. Scratches streaked his muddy legs.

He held her away from him and ran his hands down her body, looking for cuts and scrapes, feeling the tremors that shook her limbs. She, too, was soaked and muddy, covered with minor scratches and bruises.

Dax pulled her into his arms and kissed her deeply, tasting rain and the sweetness that was hers alone. The fear they had both experienced exploded into passion as wild and fierce as the storm raging around them. They writhed in each other's arms, pressing closer, closer, their wet bodies clinging together.

When his mouth released hers, they stared into each other's eyes, awed by the forces shaking their bodies. Dax shook his head to clear it, then grabbed her hand, shouting over the noise.

"There's a cave in the rock face. It's not large, but it will give us some shelter." He hoped to God he was remembering correctly and this was the right area.

A long thirty minutes elapsed before he found the cave. Carrie stumbled through the wind and blackness behind him, plunging over soaked leaves and branches, shivering with a chill, ducking when lightning cracked nearby.

Dax jerked away a tangle of vines that partially obscured the cave entrance. "Inside," he gasped. The rain poured down in torrents, like a bucket upended over their heads. It was difficult to breathe.

A soft, mossy growth covered the floor of the small cave. And it was dry. The roof was low enough that neither of them could stand, but they could sit comfortably.

Dax followed Carrie inside, pushed the wet hair from her face, then pulled her into his arms, trying to warm her with his body. She clung to him, covering his throat and jaw with wet kisses, brushing the rain from his shoulders with her chilled fingers.

"Oh, Dax. I was never so glad to see anyone in my whole life!"

"Carrie. Beautiful Carrie."

His mouth found hers in the darkness, and he guided her to the floor of the cave, pressing her along the length of his body, feeling the tremors that continued to ripple over her. "Let me warm you," he said in a thick voice, rubbing his hands over her shoulders, her arms, her waist.

She moved his hand to her breast, and his heart stopped, then thundered forward. He felt the nipple straining against her wet shirt, hard against his palm. Felt her woman's body pressing against him as if she wanted to melt into his warmth and be absorbed by it.

An explosive need rocked Dax's senses. Dimly he heard the boom of thunder and the jagged sizzle of lightning. He heard his pulse drumming in his ears, heard his blood rushing through his frame. He heard Carrie's quickened breath near his ear, heard her groan his name in a throaty whisper.

Fingers flying with urgency, she pulled at the snap on his cutoffs, helped him drag the soaked material down his body. Then his shaking hands were helping her off with her shirt and shorts, hurrying, rushing toward that moment when he could clasp her naked skin next to his. His arousal was so powerful that he ached with wanting her.

But his first need was to ground himself in the reality of this small, precious woman. He needed to taste and touch her, needed to feast his senses on the faint apricot scent of her skin, needed to warm her in the heat of his desire.

Bending over the pale gleam of her body, he waited until the sky pulsed white and the flash revealed rounded swollen breasts and the creamy flare of curving hips. Then he bent to her and licked the raindrops from between her breasts, circling his tongue toward a trembling rosy tip.

He heard her draw a sharp breath, then moan softly, felt her fingers curling in his wet hair, guiding him, informing him by touch and small murmurs what she most liked.

He kissed her feverishly, tasting the freshness of her skin, feeling her twist and grow warm beneath the fire of his passion.

"Dax..." Her hips lifted and she squirmed beneath him, reaching for his shoulders, trying to pull his mouth up to hers.

"Not yet," he murmured hoarsely.

Sliding on the mossy growth, he moved lower, brushing kisses along the length of her body. Gently he guided her legs apart, then surrounded her center with teasing kisses, pausing to blow warm breath across the crisp triangle he found.

"Dax, please." Her moan was urgent. Her fingers scrabbled on his shoulders.

His arousal throbbed and grew painful with his need for her. But first . . . He lowered his mouth to her center and tasted deep of her, tasted her own liquid need.

Only after her hips lifted in an involuntary invitation, only after he heard her gasp deeply and cry out his name, only after she began to thrash and almost sob in her urgency did he rise from her honeyed sweetness and lift over her, claiming her mouth with his lips as he thrust into her.

They came together with a cataclysmic wildness that mirrored the storm raging beyond the cave's small entrance. They rolled on the soft moss, thrusting and pulling at each other, nipping and scratching, gasping and breathless with a passion that seemed to rock the earth beneath them.

Once Dax looked down at her as a bolt of lightning split the sky. Her throat was arched and her eyes were closed. She wore an expression so radiant with pleasure that he wanted the moment to endure forever. He wanted to sink himself deep into her mystery and never emerge.

When he finally felt her shudder beneath him and cry out, when he had spent himself, Dax dropped to her side, panting and gasping, an arm across her breasts, one leg across her hips.

It seemed an age before they finally caught their breath and Carrie stirred, moving to nestle her head in the curve of his shoulder. She rested her cheek against his chest.

"I'm sorry I ran away," she murmured. "It was a stupid, juvenile thing to do."

He stroked her hair, gazing past her shoulder to the entrance of the cave. The lightning flashes came with less frequency. The rolls of thunder seemed quieter and more distant. The rain had diminished to a gentle patter.

"It was my fault." His arms tightened around her. "I said some terrible things to you, Carrie. I apologize."

"I'm the one who should apologize, and I do." She drew circles on his chest with her forefinger. "I knew I shouldn't read your manuscript, but I did it anyway. And about what I said later—"

"Carrie—"

"No, let me finish. I was out of line, Dax. You were right. I'm just a hack reporter, I'm not a psychologist. I had no right to make those comments about . . . you know. I'm sorry. Nothing is simple in today's world. There are probably a lot of reasons you're having difficulty writing."

Gently Dax eased her out of his arms and onto the moss. He sat up and looked at her face, waiting for another lightning flash so she could see that he meant what he was about to say.

"There's only one reason, Carrie. And I'm embarrassed that I didn't recognize it myself."

He leaned forward and wrapped his arms around his raised knees, speaking slowly.

"After you left the beach, I considered everything you said. I didn't want to accept it. But it was impossible to ignore the truth any longer."

Carrie started to speak, but he touched her hip and she fell silent.

"I always imagined that someday I would have a large family like the one I grew up in. I accepted it as a given that I would." He fell silent a moment. "Men don't sit around stag parties discussing the joys of parenthood. Society considers women the gender that focuses on children. Does it surprise you that I've always wanted to have children of my own?"

"A little," Carrie admitted after a pause. "The longer I know you the less surprising it seems."

"My oldest sister had her first baby when I was fifteen. I think that's when I first started thinking about the future and a family of my own." He pushed a hand through his hair, mildly surprised to discover it was dry. "My dad was a trial attorney. He left for work before we were awake. Often he didn't return until after we were in bed. Don't misunderstand, we knew we were loved. My dad was a good father. When he was there."

"But there must have been moments..."

Dax nodded. "One of the appeals of being a writer is working at home. I liked the idea that I'd be there as my kids were growing up, that I wouldn't miss any part of the process. I would have the opportunity to really know my kids, and they would know me. I planned to take an active role in raising them. Looking back, I can see that a lot of the things I've done in my life were geared toward the expectation of having a family some day."

"Dax...I don't know what to say."

"You said it on the beach, and I thank God that you did." He turned toward her, unable to see her expression. "I thought I'd dealt with it, Carrie. I honestly believed that. In fact, I thought I'd accepted my sterility rather well. Instead, I only submerged the disappointment and pain. I pushed the knowledge down to some place where I didn't have to think about it or face it. I told myself it was okay that I'd never have a wife or a family. Shrugged it off like it was no big deal."

"Isn't that a shortsighted view? There are lots of terrific divorcees and widows who come with a ready-made family..."

"I genuinely like children, and yes, I might learn to like someone else's children. But love them?" He shook his head. "I honestly don't think I could love another man's children. Certainly not like I would love my own. And that wouldn't be fair to anyone involved. Maybe that's selfish or stubborn, but that's how I feel." He paused, and something new came into his voice, something tentative and almost shy, almost a question. "If I'm going to have a wife or any kind of long-term relationship...it has to be with a woman who for some reason doesn't want or can't have children."

Carrie sat up and moved away from him. Dax sensed a sudden tension between them that hadn't been there a few minutes ago. She was silent for several moments, uncharacteristic for Carrie.

"Are you saying that now you're okay with your sterility?" she asked in a low, tentative voice.

He smiled, wishing it was that easy. "I'm saying that I've stopped hiding from myself, thanks to your honesty. Dealing with the issue is going to be a long process. But I've made a beginning. I think the writing will start to come easier as I begin to accept a different vision of myself and the future." He drew a breath. "It's going to be okay."

"I'm glad, Dax."

Turning, he reached for her in the darkness, speaking earnestly and with gratitude. "God knows what might have happened to my career if you hadn't forced the issue by being so open and honest. I might have ended up blocked and a has-been without ever recognizing what went wrong. From the bottom of my heart, I thank you for being honest enough to say the tough things other people don't have the courage to say. You're a very special person, Carrie. I admire and respect you as much as I have ever admired or respected anyone."

Carrie dropped her head and squirmed away from him. "Please," she said in a low voice. "Don't say anything more."

"I don't understand." Frowning, he tried to see her face in the dim light. "I'm trying to tell you that you were right. I was being a hypocrite. The thing I admire most is honesty, yet I was being dishonest with myself. Your honesty and clear vision saw through that. I'm trying to thank you for having the courage to speak honestly and—"

Her hands flew up to cover her ears. "Stop it!"

"Carrie, what's wrong?" He reached for her, but she pushed his hands away. "What—"

"I haven't been honest with you!"

Dax heard the tears in her voice. When his hands brushed her shoulders, she was trembling. "What's wrong? Did I say something to upset you? I don't—"

"Haven't you noticed that I'm gaining weight?"

"Carrie..." It seemed to him that she changed the subject with a bewildering abruptness that left him far behind. He didn't have the faintest notion what she was talking about.

"I don't have a waistline anymore!"

Her voice puzzled him, a strange mixture of anger, despair and tears. He reached for her again, but she pushed him away.

"We've been together almost two months. Didn't you once ever wonder if I was having a period or how I was managing the lack of proper equipment?"

A sudden stillness fell over him. "I never thought about it."

"Dax...I'm pregnant."

Chapter Eleven

At dawn's first light they crawled out of the small cave. Dax led them through the dripping foliage to the house. They climbed over the fallen tree blocking the staircase, then silently surveyed the storm damage inside.

Strong winds had blown out two of the windows. Broken glass covered the kitchen counter and some of the living room furniture. One of the drapes had been torn away from the rod. Several pieces of the light wicker furniture were overturned, and twigs, leaves and loose manuscript pages littered every surface.

Norman and a few favored pals had sought refuge inside, leaving behind feathers, seed snacks and droppings.

"My God. What a mess," Carrie murmured, looking around her. She turned one of the wicker chairs upright, found and inspected the seat cushion, looking for water damage. It was dry. Most of the water damage had occurred near the windows.

"The generator's out. I'll have to tinker with it."

"While you do that, I'll get started in here."

Dax shook his head. Bending, he brushed leaves and manuscript pages off the sofa cushions. "Sit down first. There's something... Why didn't you tell me earlier?"

She didn't have to ask what he referred to. Not looking at him, Carrie took a chair facing the deck. Outside the foliage, even the air, glistened and sparkled in the first full rays of sunlight. A damp, fertile scent permeated every breath. As the sun rose and the temperature climbed, shimmering steam wafted off the warming earth.

"I didn't remember myself for several weeks," she said finally. "I blocked it out." She glanced at his expressionless face, then away. "Talk about hiding from yourself." After another pause, she reluctantly continued. "Then, when I did remember, I was devastated. I had a hard time accepting that it was really true. I'm still resisting." She bit her lip and closed her eyes.

After a long moment she spoke again. "Hours go by, then suddenly I remember. A wave of rejection comes up in my throat and I think, no, I'm not ready for this. I'll get pregnant later, when my life is more settled." She rubbed her forehead. "Like the whole thing will go away if I tell myself often enough that the time isn't right now."

"How long have you known you were pregnant? When did you remember?"

Carrie placed a hand on her stomach. She kept her gaze on the bright sky outside the open door. "From the very beginning I knew there was something... but I didn't want to remember. Then, that day when you swam out to the boat, when you told me your secret..." She covered her eyes with a hand. "I should have guessed much, much earlier. My breasts are larger, and so is my stomach. I don't have a waist anymore. I can't close the top button of my shorts."

"Damn it, Carrie. You should have told me immediately!"

She was silent for a full minute. "By the time I had to face what's happening to my body, you and I... I guess I thought if you knew I was pregnant, things wouldn't... we wouldn't..."

He nodded shortly and looked at his clasped hands. "You're right. I don't think we would have let things go this far."

They both watched Norman hop through the doorway, cock a bright eye at the mess, then hop out as if he disapproved of their housekeeping. Neither of them smiled.

"It's Michael's baby," Dax said after a lengthy silence. It wasn't a question.

Carrie nodded, suddenly feeling too tired to lift her hand. "That's what the final big fight was about. I remember that now, too. Michael wanted me to get an abortion. I refused. That's when he told me that he was married. I stomped out and climbed into the rubber boat. The rest, as they say, is history."

"How far along are you?"

"As near as I can figure, about four and a half months."

Dax leaned over and pushed both hands through his hair. "I don't know what to say. I need to think about this."

Carrie drew a deep breath, then shifted in the chair to look at him. "This has nothing to do with you,

Dax," she said softly. "You don't need to worry. I have no expectations, I'm not looking for anything from you. We both know when the supply plane leaves here, I'll be on it. Very likely we'll never see each other again."

He stared straight ahead, looking at the storm debris that littered the bed. Standing abruptly, he strode toward the door.

"I'll see if I can get the generator up and running. With any luck, we should be able to cook breakfast in about an hour." He didn't look at her as he passed her chair. "Can't have you missing any meals. You're eating for two now."

Bitterness and anger put an edge on his voice.

Carrie watched him go. His image shimmered behind a blur of tears.

EVERYTHING CHANGED.

To Dax's surprise, the changes in his professional life delighted him.

To begin, he invited Carrie to the final-manuscript burning on the beach.

"I hate to see you destroy your work. Are you sure about this?" she asked doubtfully, watching him feed the pages of his book into the flames.

"I'm positive," Dax said firmly, watching flakes of paper ash float toward the evening sky. "I've got a new story brewing in here—" he tapped his forehead "—that's gonna knock your socks off. If you aren't scared out of your wits by page twenty, I'll bite your neck myself."

"Sounds good to me," Carrie said with a roguish roll of her eyes. Instantly she stiffened and turned aside with a stricken expression. Neither of them could think of anything to say for several minutes.

"Well," Dax said finally, his voice artificially hearty. "I brought weiners and marshmallows. How about putting a couple of hot dogs on those sticks while I build up the fire?"

The moment passed.

The change he liked best was discussing his work with Carrie. Her input was proving invaluable.

"You're really good at editing," he said the next day, studying her latest comments.

She smiled across the dinner table. "Thanks for letting me be part of the process."

Dax lifted his head and stared at her. "Are you kidding? You have great instincts. Haven't I taken all of your suggestions?"

"Eventually," she replied with a smile. "Occasionally it's been touch and go. You're pretty intimidating when you're angry."

He rolled his eyes and pushed his empty plate aside. "Ever since I met you, I've been trying to intimidate you into doing things my way. Has it ever worked? One time?"

"We pushy types are hard to steamroll." Her smile widened. "Look, that new scene is burning in your brain. Why don't you go back to work?"

His fingers flew over the keyboard, his thoughts happily focused. Now that he was writing the kind of book he was meant to write, excited by a good story, he'd regained his concentration.

Professionally, he had never been happier. Personally... well, that was a different story. Personally, things were far more complicated.

THE DISTANCING BEGAN the night of the storm, the night Carrie told him about the baby.

When Dax wasn't thinking about the new book, he thought about Carrie being pregnant. And he thought about Michael Medlin. He would love to have gotten his hands on the bastard. He would have pounded Medlin into pulp and taken great satisfaction in doing it. Medlin had deceived her, then sidestepped his responsibility with a shrug and the suggestion that Carrie abort his baby.

Dax ran along the shore, scattering a colony of sand crabs and a flock of sea gulls.

Jealousy burned in his chest. Under no circumstances would Dax ever have agreed to abort a child of his. If Carrie's baby had been sired by him, he would have married her the instant he learned about the pregnancy. He would have been thrilled to learn such a fine woman carried his child.

Approaching runner's euphoria, he pictured what his child would look like. It would be dark-haired, of course. He hoped it would have Carrie's sparkling emerald eyes. If it was a boy, he wouldn't mind if he grew up with Dax's build. And he liked his chin. Carrie's nose would be perfect if the child was a girl.

God. What was he thinking of? Stopping short, he leaned his hands on his knees and fought to catch his breath.

It wasn't his child. It would never be his child. Carrie was pregnant with Michael Medlin's child.

And Dax for damned sure didn't want anything to do with another man's baby.

Because he didn't want any misunderstandings between himself and Carrie, he withdrew from her physically, though he ached for her. Some nights he lay in his hammock listening to her toss and turn on the bed and he wanted her so much that he thought he would burst. Occasionally he worked off his desire with a midnight run on the beach. Other times he prowled the dark house, pacing and wishing Carrie had never come into his life.

"Dax?" Her pillow rustled as she pushed up in bed. "Why aren't you asleep?"

There was enough moonlight that he could see she was wearing one of his shirts. It pulled over her stomach. In the last couple of weeks, her stomach had expanded to the point that even a kid would have known she was pregnant.

"I'm just restless tonight. Go back to sleep."

But she mounded the pillows against the headboard and folded her hands on her stomach, silently watching him pace.

He sat down and dropped his head in his hands. He might as well talk about it. "When you get back to Denver, are you going to contact Michael? Will you tell him about the baby?"

"No. Not a chance." She was quiet, moving her hands gently across her stomach. "Michael was a mistake. A bad mistake." She released a breath. "He has his life—I have mine. I don't ever want to see him again. Michael gave up any right to this child when he threw some money at me and told me to get an abortion."

Dax stroked his temples and ground his teeth. He could imagine that final scene as vividly as if he'd been present.

"Dax?" Her voice sounded hesitant and very small. "Do you hate me?"

"What?" His head snapped up.

"It's so confusing sometimes. When we're talking about your writing, I feel close to you. Like we're thinking the same thoughts, almost. But the rest of the time, you seem so far away."

He rubbed a hand over his jaw and tilted his head to gaze at the ceiling fan. "I don't hate you, Carrie."

"The supply plane should arrive next week. I'd like to think that you and I are going to part as friends."

He heard the pain in her voice and felt his own chest constrict. It occurred to him that the island was going to be very quiet and very lonely after Carrie departed. Suddenly he imagined a clock ticking inside his chest, counting down the hours left to them.

Going to the bed, he stretched out beside her and guided her into his arms. She snuggled down next to him and laid her cheek on his shoulder.

"Of course we're friends."

He stroked her hair, thinking what a wonderful mother she was going to be. Loving, nurturing, involved. Carrie's child would learn honesty in the cradle, would possess a healthy sense of confidence and self-esteem. Her child would grow up surrounded by love and laughter and encouragement and good advice. Everything a child needed.

Except a father.

"You have to know I'm not marriage material, Carrie. I've been up front about that. I'm a loner, always have been. Keeping that in mind helps me accept my sterility, in fact." He had to say it, just in case she'd been fantasizing about solutions.

She didn't say anything.

"We've made some short-term compromises, but you and I are opposites in a lot of ways. You're a night person, I'm a day person. And there are other examples. You know what I mean."

She moved a hand up to her eyes, but he couldn't tell if she was crying.

He tightened his arms around her and rested his chin on top of her head, staring into the darkness. "All right, look. Maybe if things had been different... But I can't help how I feel. Some men can accept another man's children and love them like their own. But I'm not that kind of man. I couldn't make that kind of situation work. I'd always resent it that—"

"Please, Dax, we've covered this. I know how you feel."

He didn't think so. Did she know that he still wanted her? Did she know that he looked at her and felt himself go weak inside because she grew more radiant and more beautiful every day? Did she guess that he dreaded the arrival of the supply plane or that he missed her already?

He continued to hold her long after she fell asleep, listening to her quiet breathing and feeling her stomach pressing against his side. He wanted a glass of Scotch in the worst way, but he didn't move.

"DO YOU REALIZE you don't own a single book about pregnancy or taking care of babies?" Carrie stood in front of the bookshelves, hands on hips, a frown tugging her mouth. "But then, I guess there's no reason you would."

"Mmm?"

"The only thing we have is the encyclopedia. It's better than nothing, but I wish we had something more detailed and specific." She pulled a volume off the shelf. "I'm going to rest in the hammock and read. Lunch is in the fridge."

"Mmm."

"Dax?" she called. "Your hair is on fire."

"Okay."

Smiling, Carrie shooed Norman out of the doorway, then settled herself in the hammock and propped the encyclopedia volume against her nonexistent waist. She read about the changes taking place in her body with great interest and not a little awe.

It was still difficult to accept that she was going to have a baby. She had been in denial for so long. Occasionally a wave of recognition and shock would roll over her, so intense that she had to sit down and fight to catch her breath.

Her breasts were tender and sensitive. Her stomach and waist seemed to be expanding at an alarming rate. And she'd been experiencing a strong nesting urge. She felt an almost compulsive need to rearrange Dax's kitchen and put his house in order.

Her expression sobered, thinking about Dax. When he wasn't keeping her at arm's length, he treated her as if she were as fragile as an egg. She had to continually remind him that she was pregnant, not infirm. She could do all the things she had done before.

Dax. The days were counting down. Soon now, the supply plane would arrive to drop fresh provisions, discover the red distress flag and send help. Their interlude together would end. Dax would remain here to finish his book. Carrie would return to the States and try to glue together the tattered fragments of her life.

Alone.

"CARRIE? Is something wrong?"

He had to call her name twice before she heard him, then she jumped, startled, and lifted her head.

Dax turned off the computer and walked toward the counter. "You've been standing in the kitchen staring at that cup of coffee for twenty minutes."

She moved aside as he opened the fridge and removed a cold beer. "You're not able to work today?"

Dax slid onto one of the stools, popped the can and studied her face. "I don't think I've ever seen you looking so down in the mouth. Talk to me, Carrie. Are you feeling all right?"

"I'm fine." She poured out the cold coffee, chose a glass of cold instant milk instead.

"No, you're not. You're never this quiet."

She leaned toward the window. A steady rain dripped against the tropical foliage. The air felt heavy with humidity and the perfume of tropical blossoms. "I'm a little low in my mind. That's all."

He nodded, a slight frown pulling his brow. "You're young and healthy. You're going to deliver a fine baby. Nothing will go wrong."

"I'm not worrying about that. It's all the other stuff."

"Like?" he asked, prodding her.

Carrie sighed and came around the counter to sit on a stool beside him, propping her chin in the palm of her hand.

"I'm not sure what I'm going to do." She paused and sighed again. "Maybe I'll go to Galveston, spend some time with my parents." Biting her lip, she watched the warm rain slanting past the window. "Eventually I'll have to decide where I'm going to live and how." She shrugged, feeling more depressed by the minute. "My biggest worry is that I don't have a job anymore. How am I going to support myself and little Who's-it?"

"I've been doing some thinking, too," Dax admitted, examining the Coors can. "I'd like to help out. I may have some problems, but money isn't one of them. I have more money than I'll ever spend. I don't think you should try to find a job until a couple of months after the baby is born."

Carrie pushed back on the stool and stared at him. "I can't take your money, Dax. This isn't your problem."

"I know. But I want to help."

"You don't owe me anything."

He glared at her. "That isn't the point. We're friends, aren't we? Can't one friend help another in a time of need?"

"Not if it means supporting that friend and her baby for several months. Even if I cut corners and counted every penny, do you know how much that would cost?" She waved a hand, getting upset. "An apartment, furniture, transportation, food, utilities, a phone. We're talking thousands of dollars, Dax."

"Damn it, I told you. Money is no problem. So it costs several thousand dollars, so what?"

"So how could I repay a loan like that? What if the best job I can find only pays a pittance?"

He rolled his eyes in irritation. "I'm not talking about a loan," he said, striving for patience.

Her chin rose, nudged by pride and a set of unbending standards. "The only way I would accept financial help is if it came on the basis of a loan with a note payable at the going rate of interest."

Dax threw up his hands. "Fine. If that's the only way you'll let someone help you, then fine. We'll make it a loan."

Frustrated tears shadowed her eyes. "Which brings us back to square one. You know how little journalism pays. And I'm not even particularly good at the job. I don't see how I could repay a loan. So thanks, but no thanks."

"Sometimes you drive me absolutely crazy." His fingers gripped the can of beer. "You have a problem, I'm offering a solution. Why are you making this difficult?"

"Look, Dax. In a few days I'm going to leave here and you and I will never see each other again." Color flooded her cheeks. "Oh, maybe we'll phone each other on occasion after you finish the book and return to Manhattan. We might exchange a line at Christmas for a year or two. But that will be the extent of it."

"Carrie—"

"You'll be in New York, and I'll be somewhere else. I'll build a new life for me and the baby, and you'll go on with your life. Our paths are not going to cross. Every now and then I'll see you on a television interview and I'll remember these months on the island. Every now and then you'll run across a pushy reporter and you may think of me. But when I leave here, that's the end. We'll never see each other again!''

She stared at him a moment, then she burst into tears and ran into the bathroom, slamming the door behind her.

Dax looked at his can of beer. The countdown clock ticking in his chest seemed very loud.

HE DIDN'T FIND the sticky note on the refrigerator until he stopped for lunch and started rummaging in the kitchen for a can of Spam.

When you're ready for a break, come to the grotto.

Dax started out the door, then returned to the house for a tube of sun block. She never remembered sun block. While he was at it, he mixed a pitcher of lemonade and tucked two plastic tumblers under his arm. She didn't drink enough liquids, either.

He followed the path that Carrie had partially rebuilt before the storm that brought so many changes. It occurred to him there was no part of the island on which she hadn't left a mark.

When he stepped into the clearing of the grotto, he was overwhelmed with memories of the day he had found her floating naked among the flower petals. That moment, and the lovemaking that followed, he would remember all his life.

When he saw Carrie sitting on the edge of the pool, dangling her bare legs in the water, he stopped short. She had remembered to wear one of his hats and had pushed her hair up beneath it, but her head was down, the nape of her neck exposed. That small patch of skin between hairline and shirt collar looked so fragile and vulnerable that he felt a sudden pain in his chest. She looked so small and miserable and alone.

He cleared his throat and watched her shoulders straighten. He could almost see her arranging a smile on her lips before she turned to look at him over her shoulder.

"Hi. I brought some sun block." Her nose had started to redden. "And some lemonade."

"Great. Lemonade sounds wonderful." While he poured, she smiled and rubbed sun block on her nose and cheeks. Then she patted the rock next to her. "I saved you a seat."

They drank the lemonade in silence, looking at the water lapping their feet.

"I guess you're curious as to why I called this meeting," Carrie said when she couldn't stand the silence another second. She wondered if Dax guessed the effect it had on her to sit this close to him. She could feel the heat of his large body, imagined that she felt his strength and vitality wrapping around her.

She wondered if he could hear her heart crumbling and cracking off in little pieces.

"Do we need a reason to share a glass of lemonade?" He lifted his head toward the water spilling down the rock face.

Carrie pushed a piece of ice around the edges of her glass. "The supply plane should arrive tomorrow."

"I fixed the flagpole after the storm. The pilot should have no trouble seeing the red distress signal."

"How long after that will it take for help to arrive?"

He shrugged, still studying the waterfall. "A couple of hours. Not much more. My guess is the pilot will send back a heliocopter."

Carrie nodded, gripping her glass in both hands. "Things will probably get a little hectic after the heliocopter arrives." She drew a breath. "I've never been much good at goodbyes. I always feel hurried and a little frantic, and I never really say what I later wished I had."

"I know what you mean. I'm not good with goodbyes, either."

"So I thought I'd say goodbye now." She felt him turn to stare at her, but she kept her eyes focused on the glass of lemonade, glad he'd brought it. "I want you to know that I'll never forget this island, or you. I'll always remember these months no matter what else happens in my life. Knowing you has been... I've learned so many things about myself, thanks to you. I've learned I don't want to go back to newspaper work. And I think I've learned how to compromise, how to live with another person." She lifted her head and met his eyes. "That reminds me. You know I'm not going to tell anyone where you are. You do know that, don't you?"

"It doesn't matter anymore."

"The new book is wonderful, Dax. It's the best work you've ever done. If the reviewers don't rave about this one, well, you can tell them for me that they're full of crap. My only regret is that I won't be able to read the last half until it appears in the bookstores."

"When it's finished, I'll send you a copy of the final draft," he said in a hoarse voice.

"I'd like that." She dropped her head. "Damn it, I'm just not good at this. I want to tell you that I admire you and that I've loved being here with you and that I'm going to miss you like an amputated limb." Tears glistened on her lashes. "I wanted to say that you're a good, decent man. Beneath all that bluster, you're kind and gentle and generous. I want to tell you that I love you but I can't think of a way to do it where you won't think I'm looking for some kind of declaration from you. Which I'm not. But, Dax..." She raised her head and looked at him with swimming eyes. "I do love you. You're one of the best friends I've ever had. I may never see you again after tomorrow. But I'll never forget you."

His big hands closed on her shoulders, turning her to face him.

"Meeting you has changed my life, Carrie. I was running full blast down the wrong path. Now you and that damned honesty of yours—" leaning over, he peered under her hat brim, trying to coax a smile "—have made it possible for me to work again. To live again. You'll never know what these last three months have meant to me. I'll never forget you and all that I owe you."

"You don't owe me anything, Dax."

He was quiet a minute. "That's just like you. You work miracles, then brush aside any compliment. I've never known anyone as remarkable as you are, Carrie James. I wonder sometimes if you realize how strong you are. I've never heard you complain, never heard a word of self-pity pass your lips. You don't hold grudges, don't look back. I'm going to miss you,

Carrie. It's going to seem awfully quiet around here without you. I love you, too, my friend."

Carrie suppressed a wince. She didn't want him to love her like a friend. She wanted him to love her heart and soul, with passion and fire. Like she loved him.

She made herself lift her head and meet his dark eyes through the tears swimming in her own. "Goodbye, Dax." She couldn't manage anything louder than a whisper. "I'll never forget you."

"Goodbye, Carrie," he said softly. He blinked rapidly as if he had something in his eye.

Carrie leaned her forehead against his and closed her eyes. A tear rolled down her cheek. She wondered if anyone had ever died from a broken heart. "This is so hard. I hate goodbyes."

"So do I," he said in a gruff voice.

Dax slipped his arm around her waist, and she leaned her head against his shoulder. They sat in silence, watching the waterfall and waiting for tomorrow.

BECAUSE SHE COULDN'T BEAR to remain in the house twitching every time she heard a sound that might be the plane, Carrie decided to wait on the beach.

"Put on some sun block before you go," Dax said. He sat in front of his computer, but he wasn't typing. He looked as tired as she did, as if he hadn't slept last night, either.

"I'll come and get you when I see the plane," she said, almost running out the door.

It was a relief to get away from him. Every time she looked at Dax, a spasm of pain tightened her chest. Carrie had believed she had been in love before, but now she knew she had never really loved a man before Dax. Comparing what she had felt before to what she felt for Dax was like comparing a breeze to a hurricane.

Walking through the gently rolling surf, she watched a half dozen long-tailed birds picking at feathery strings of seaweed and listened to the silky whisper of waves rolling up the beach.

It would seem strange to return to wool slacks and sweaters, coats and gloves and heavy, waterproof footwear.

Dreading the moment of departure with all her heart, but wanting to get it over with, she bit her lip and scanned the sky. The plane could appear at any minute. As there was no landing strip on the island, the pilot would do a low fly-by, check the color of the flag on the pole, then he would return to Elesia, the nearest populated island, and send help at once.

When the end came, it would happen swiftly. Within an hour of the rescue helicopter's arrival Carrie would be lifted into the sky, winging home to pick up the pieces of her life.

A tear rolled down her tanned cheek and dropped into the surf. Feeling more miserable than she'd imagined a person could feel, she dashed at the tears slipping down her face. She blinked at the sky, wishing the damned plane would appear.

Her heart was breaking. She was dying inside.

"Carrie!"

Wiping furiously at the tears on her cheeks, she lifted her head and saw Dax race onto the beach, pause to look along the shore, then sprint toward her. The expression on his face momentarily paralyzed her.

Something was terribly wrong. Carrie had never seen fear on Dax's face before, or uncertainty. His deep tan had paled to a gray color.

Heart pounding, she ran forward and met him at the waterline, gripping his forearms and peering into his face.

"What's happened? What is it, Dax?"

He pulled her roughly into his arms, knocking her hat off, crushing her so tightly against him that she heard his heart hammering in his chest, felt a tremble shaking his big body.

Fright stiffened Carrie's body. She couldn't begin to imagine what had done this to him.

"Dax. Dax, what is it?" Pushing a little away, she tried to see his face. His eyes were closed and he was holding her fiercely, almost desperately, like she was a lifeline, like she was the only thing holding him together right now.

His hands moved over her body as if he was reassuring himself that she was real and still here. Warm fingers stroked her arms, her back, the nape of her neck, her loose hair. Finally he cupped her face and gazed into her eyes with an intensity that made her heart skip a beat.

"I can't let this happen. I can't let you fly out of my life. I love you, Carrie!"

"What?" she whispered, hardly daring to breathe.

"I love you, and I don't mean like a friend." His fingers tightened on her shoulders. He was shaking. "I don't want a life without you. When the helicopter comes, I'm going with you."

"Dax—"

"No, just listen a minute. The answer to everything is for us to get married. It solves the financial problems, and the baby will have a name."

"Married?" She gaped at him. Her heart lurched, then soared into her throat.

"I'm going to try to be easier to live with, Carrie, I promise. I'll keep regular hours, I'll try not to be as moody. I'll try to be as giving as you are. And maybe in time you'll learn to love me as much as I love you."

She lifted on her tiptoes, caught his face between her hands and kissed him over and over, covering his beloved face with a shower of kisses. He held her so tightly she thought her bones would crack.

"You idiot. I love you, too. Oh, God, Dax. I love you so much that sometimes I think I'll explode with loving you!"

"I want to spend the rest of my life with you. Life wouldn't be worthwhile without you in it. You fill an emptiness I didn't even know I felt!"

He kissed her so hard that he took her breath away and left her trembling. Wrapping his arms around her, he crushed her against his body.

"When I ran down here to find you, I was so afraid the plane might already have come and I was minutes away from losing you. I can't stand that thought, Carrie. I don't ever want to spend a day away from you. I need you so much. I don't ever want to say goodbye to you!"

She threw herself on him so unexpectedly that they tumbled down on the sand and the waves washed over their legs. Laughing and crying, Carrie covered his face with kisses.

"I love you, I love you, I love you! I think I loved you even when I thought you were a Neanderthal. Oh, Dax, I love you so damned much!"

A deep hunger exploded between them. They kissed each other frantically, urgently, almost with frustration, as if kisses were not enough.

They dropped to their knees in the surf, lips clinging as water swirled around their waists. Carrie's vision shrank to include only him. She saw the dark shadows on his cheeks, ran her lips over unshaved stubble, dug her fingers into the smooth, bronzed perfection of his shoulders.

"I love the look of you," she murmured helplessly. The sunlight shining in his hair, the golden flecks in his brown eyes. She loved the way his expressive mouth softened when he laughed, grew firm when he was annoyed or tired. She loved the way he moved on the balls of his feet, fluid, with the grace and beauty of a natural athlete. She even loved the scent of him and would have recognized it anywhere, a combination of soap and sunshine and something else that reminded her of leather and new schoolbooks.

Dax was the most splendid man she had ever known, proud and strong, beautiful in his masculine power and vitality. She would remember him always as he was now, darkly intense, passion blazing in eyes turned almost black by desire.

Fiery kisses burned over her throat, her lips, her eyelids. She heard him swear as he fought to kick out of his cutoffs, struggled with the buttons on her shirt. She couldn't help him because she couldn't take her hands away from his chest, his face.

He gripped the edges of the shirt she was wearing and ripped them apart, sending buttons flying into the water bubbling around them. Finally they were both naked, half in and half out of the water, locked together by lips and bodies, gasping with the force of their hunger for each other.

Unaware of the sun and the surf, unaware of anything but their passion for each other, they made wild, frantic love on the beach, tumbling in the foaming surf, murmuring each other's names and words of love that had been old when the beach was new.

"My God," Carrie whispered, blinking at him. Her hair was wet and sandy. A rosy flush glowed on her skin. Only now did she become aware of the sand beneath her, the water ebbing and flowing over the lower half of their bodies.

"I didn't hurt you, did I?" Dax whispered. Tenderly he brushed a strand of wet hair from her cheek.

She wrapped her arms around his neck and pulled him to her for a long kiss. "We'll never get the sand off of us."

"Come on." He helped her to her feet and, naked, they ran into the cove waters. Like children, they washed the sand from each other, then chased after naked buttocks and legs, not wanting to drift farther away than a hand could reach.

When they ran out of the water, shaking drops from their hair, Carrie laughed and scooped up her clothing.

"What if the plane had come when we were..." A happy blush raised a tint of rose beneath her tanned cheeks.

Dax caught her in his arms and grinned. "The pilot would have said I was the luckiest man alive."

They both looked at the sky, half expecting the plane to swoop out of the clouds that were gathering for the afternoon rain.

Ten days later they were still waiting. That evening, Dax looked into Carrie's worried eyes across the dinner table and said aloud what they both were thinking.

"Something is very wrong."

Chapter Twelve

Carrie poured a tumbler of iced tea, then tucked herself into the corner of the sofa, adjusting the cushion to support her back. Dax sat on the other end facing her over his after-dinner coffee. He seemed to be studying her bare legs, but his expression had turned inward. She could almost hear the wheels turning as he sorted through possibilities.

"Did the first supply drop arrive when it was supposed to?" Carrie asked finally, her anxious eyes examining his face.

"Yes." Leaning forward, he placed his cup and saucer on the coffee table, then rubbed a hand over his jaw. "I'm sorry, Carrie. This is my fault." He swore softly, then struck a fist on his knee. "Cutting myself off with no form of outside communication was a damned idiotic thing to do! I should have signaled the first supply plane and told the pilot I needed another radio."

"Dax—" His expression alarmed her.

"What the hell was I trying to prove?" Standing, he paced behind the sofa. "I don't even remember, that's the stupid part. Being totally isolated seemed romantic in the archaic sense of adventure. A test of some kind. Just me and the elements. That's a laugh, isn't it?"

"There's no sense beating yourself for something you can't change." Anxiously, she watched him pace, his face dark.

He lifted his hands and scowled. "I had this house built with all the comforts. I stocked the storehouse with enough supplies to withstand a siege. Then told myself I was roughing it. What a joke!" A harsh sound of disgust rumbled from his chest. "How could I have been so stupid?"

Carrie lifted a hand as he paced past her, gazing at him with a worried frown. "Don't be so hard on yourself. Living without companionship and communication is roughing it."

"And dangerous," he said, staring at her. "You recognized the risks immediately." He drew a deep breath. "It's worse than you remember. Mort Lewan is the only person who knows where we are."

A chill gripped Carrie's chest, and for an instant she felt paralyzed. They gazed at each other in tense silence.

When Carrie could breathe again, she released a long, slow breath and spoke in a flat voice, struggling to appear calm. "So if something happened to Mort Lewan, no one would know where we are. No one would arrange for the supply plane. No one would know about the signal with the flag..." Her voice trailed off as the implications slammed home. Trying to ignore her heart hammering in her chest, Carrie gazed into her iced tea. "We may be in real trouble."

Kneeling in front on her, Dax wrapped his arms around her waist and buried his head in her lap. "I'm so sorry, Carrie. God, I'm sorry for putting us in this mess!"

She stroked his hair, loving him so hard that she ached with an inner intensity. They sat together in close silence for several minutes before the oven timer buzzed.

"There's a Sara Lee pie in the oven," Carrie announced, standing. "How does a slice of hot apple pie sound?"

"How can you eat when we're talking about being genuinely marooned?" Dax demanded, staring at her in amazement.

She patted her stomach and managed a grin. "You said it first. I'm eating for two, remember?" A shrug lifted the shoulders of the oversize shirt she had borrowed from his closet. "Marooned or not, life goes on. We have to eat."

Drawing a deep, steadying breath, she walked into the kitchen and removed the pie from the oven, then sliced it, using the time to fight the panic whirling in her brain.

"Here," she said, returning to the sofa and giving him a plate. Her voice sounded brisk and firm, almost normal. "Okay, we've had all the breast-beating and mea culpa we're going to have. Agreed? It doesn't matter how we got into this situation. What matters is how we handle it, what we do from here on out. Let's concentrate on that problem, all right?"

Dax stared at her. "You are simply amazing, do you know that?"

She smiled. "Now that's the kind of talk I like."

"Seriously. You're the most fabulous, most astonishing woman I've ever met." His dark eyes glowed with gratitude and admiration. "You're fearless!"

"No," Carrie corrected quickly. "Not fearless." They looked at each other over the plates of pie. "Just practical." Leaning forward, she placed her hand gently on his cheek. "There's no point rehashing something we can't change. What matters is how we deal with the situation."

Turning his head, he caught her hand and placed a kiss in her palm. His voice was husky. "I love you, Carrie."

"So," she said, drawing strength from the emotion shaking his deep voice, "let's consider the worst-case scenario first." She drew a deep breath, wishing she really were fearless. "Suppose no one ever rescues us and we're stuck here for the rest of our lives."

"That isn't likely," Dax said promptly, putting her worst fear to rest. "The island isn't in the path of any shipping lanes, but we're only twenty-five miles from a sizable population. The second day I was here a helicopter flew over. I assume it came from Elesia. It's possible a ship could also find us."

"You haven't seen another helicopter since?"

He shook his head and absently cut a forkful of pie. "Regretfully, no. But tomorrow I'll collect rocks and build an SOS on the beach."

"There's a couple of cans of red paint in the storehouse. We can paint the rocks so they'll stand out."

"Red paint? You're kidding!" He frowned. "Mort must have included paint on the original inventory, I didn't."

Carrie took their pie plates into the kitchen, rinsed them and placed them in the dishwasher, her mind racing.

"All right, chances are we won't be marooned for the rest of our lives. But we could be here for a long time."

Dax followed her into the kitchen and stepped behind her, his arms circling her waist. "The man who brought me out here might get curious and return to see if I'm still here. The pilot of the first supply drop also knows someone is on this island. He could get curious, too. Eventually we'll be rescued. It's only a matter of time."

She leaned against his strong big body and closed her eyes. "We'll run out of bread soon, and a few other items. But you were right, we have enough food in the freezers to last several months. We have a good supply of vitamins. We can get fresh fruit from the mango trees."

"I swear to you, Carrie, I'll get you off this island."

"We're both healthy and resourceful. We'll be fine no matter how long it takes."

Neither of them mentioned Carrie's burgeoning waist or the fact that she was now over five months pregnant. But that was the most serious worry and the one that never left their minds.

DAX GOT a severe sunburn collecting rocks and building a giant SOS on the beach. The pain was a welcome punishment for his lapse in judgment.

Although Carrie covered her ears and refused to listen to further self-flagellation, not an hour passed that he didn't berate himself for failing to flag the first supply plane, or for being so careless as to leave the deck sealant where it could spill into his ham radio and ruin it. What on earth had he been thinking of to remain here with no outside communication? Had he been so lonely and isolated that he had actually believed he would never need anyone but himself? That it didn't matter what might happen to him?

His love for Carrie was so deep that he could no longer understand his previous thinking. His reliance on and enjoyment of her was so all-encompassing that it now impressed him as incredible that he had ever rejected human warmth and companionship. He couldn't grasp that he had valued himself and his life so little that he had deliberately placed himself in a dangerous situation.

The question that ate at him with every breath he inhaled was how to rescue Carrie and her unborn baby. He had to get them off the island before the birth.

"I have an idea," he announced one evening as they relaxed on the deck watching a brilliant rainbow arch against the sunset sky. He slid a sidelong glance toward the golden glow illuminating Carrie's high cheekbones. "I've been thinking about the rubber boat."

"Me, too." After a minute she added, "But I rejected the idea. It's a very small boat—and that's a very big ocean out there."

Dax reached for her hand and held it. "It's only twenty-five miles to Elesia."

She turned to him with those steady, trusting green eyes. "I don't know diddly about navigation on the open sea. Do you?"

"That's a problem," Dax admitted. "But we have the encyclopedias." He pulled her into his lap and settled her head on his shoulder, stroking her shining hair.

"That's a scary prospect," she said in a small voice. "On-the-job training based on an encyclopedia article."

"That's why it's better if I attempt it alone." When she protested, he held her tighter, speaking over her head, staring at the sunset. "I don't want to risk you and your baby in a small boat with no shade and an inexperienced sailor."

She pushed up and looked him square in the eyes. "No, Dax. If you go, we all go." He felt a shudder tremble across her shoulders. "I couldn't stand waiting here alone, wondering what was happening to you out there."

Cupping her face, he studied her expression. "Carrie, it would be a risk. A big one. It's too dangerous for you."

Panic flared in her eyes, quivered in her voice. Her fingers tightened painfully on his shoulders. "If anything happened to you, I'd be here alone! Please, Dax, I beg you. If we have to try this, I'm going with you!"

"Shh." To calm her, he promised that he wouldn't leave her behind. But he remembered how terribly ill she had been when she washed up on his shore. Could he put her through an ordeal like that? Put her into a tiny boat on the sea with no shade and no protection?

With no guarantee that they could locate the small island of Elesia?

But if he tried it alone and if the boat capsized or if he couldn't locate Elesia, if he drifted until he was out of food and water, if he died out there, Carrie would have to deliver her baby alone with no assistance. No one on earth would know she was here and desperately in need of help.

The choice was appalling.

Closing his eyes with a grimace of pain, Dax tried to imagine why Mort had not sent the supply plane. What had gone so terribly wrong? Reason suggested the supply plane had not made the fly-by because Mort had not made the arrangements. The only logical explanation was that Mort had not made the arrangements because he couldn't.

But why? Dax tortured himself with unanswerable questions. Had Mort suffered a heart attack? Been in an accident? Was he dead?

Possibly Mort had had a stroke. Dax remembered him smoking an endless chain of imported cigars, coughing and wheezing when he walked up a set of steps. Now Dax remembered noticing an unhealthy flush the last time he had seen his agent, remembered joking about cholesterol counts and blood pressure points, recalled suggesting that Mort give up the cigars and Jack Daniels. Mort had laughed, coughed and waved the suggestion aside with a growl.

The questions were driving him crazy. The writer in him demanded a neat and tidy explanation, but there was none.

"Still want to marry me?" he asked in a gruff voice, burying his face in Carrie's hair. The chestnut tendrils smelled like sunshine and lemon shampoo.

"The sooner the better."

"We're not off to a great start."

Smiling, she lifted her face and kissed his chin. "As usual, we don't agree. How many couples get to honeymoon on a deserted romantic island? We're lucky."

Lucky, he thought as she lowered her head to his shoulder. His throat tightened. Only Carrie could turn a disaster into something optimistic. But, he conceded, he was definitely lucky. He was the luckiest man alive to have found this precious woman.

"Come to bed," he murmured gruffly in her ear, his hands stroking her back. He needed to hold her and love her, needed to show her how deeply she had touched him.

She smiled against his neck. "Before dinner? Is this a ploy? Did you forget to put anything out to thaw?"

He laughed, the sound soft and low in his throat. His lips found hers, and he kissed her deeply and tenderly. "I want to hold you and thank God for sending you to me."

Lifting her, he carried her inside and gently placed her on the bed, aching inside when she raised her arms to him. With a low groan he lay down beside her and spooned her into the curve of his body, feeling her womanly warmth and the softness of her body, inhaled the heady fragrance of her hair and skin.

Instantly his body stirred, unaware that tonight his needs ran deeper than physical gratification, although he wanted her. After a dozen lingering kisses, he slowly unbuttoned the oversize shirt she wore and gazed at her in the fading glow of sunset shadows.

Awed by her beauty, Dax tenderly cupped her breasts in his hands, exploring the increased fullness and weight, brushing light kisses across the standing tips. Her changing form delighted him and filled him with wonder. He gloried in watching the minute alterations occurring with each passing day.

Gently, almost reverently, he smoothed his large hands over the curve of her belly and fantasized that she carried his child. His chest and throat tightened in painful longing that he swallowed with difficulty, concentrating instead on tracing the blue veins that had come into prominence on her breasts. He mapped the delicate lines with a trembling finger.

Her pregnancy fascinated him. But he didn't often think about the baby itself. That was a different story. The baby was another man's child.

Tears of happiness glistened in Carrie's lovely eyes. "Sometimes I look at you and almost wish I liked Spam. That's how much I love you."

He laughed and wrapped his arms around her. "Our differences aren't nearly the problem I thought they might be. In fact, the contrasts are stimulating."

She rolled her eyes, then grinned at him, teasing. "Oh, my. You really are in love, aren't you?"

"With all my heart," he said seriously, gazing into her face. "And for the first time in my life."

Her eyebrows lifted in delight. "The first time?"

"The first and only," he said, smiling. "See, you have done the extraordinary, something no one else has ever done. You're the only woman I've ever want to marry." There had been other women, but none like this one. No woman had ever penetrated the armor shielding his heart. He had never surrendered.

Then Carrie had exploded into his life and shattered his defenses. And suddenly he had realized how lonely he was, how hungry and desperate for companionship of the heart. She had made him see that he was incomplete at the same moment that she provided the remedy. Just having her beside him fulfilled him in ways he would not have thought possible. Finally Dax understood what love was.

Leaning over her, gazing into her eyes, he tried to tell her a little of what she meant to him.

"All my life I've felt as if I was waiting for something," he said gruffly. "I didn't know what it was." Lifting a hand, he smoothed a silky strand off her brow. "That sense of waiting is gone. I was waiting for you, waiting to love and be loved, waiting for someone who would make sense out of life."

Surprise widened her eyes, and she lifted a hand to his cheek. "I've felt that, too!" Wonder made her face radiant. "And you're right—now the waiting is over! Oh, Dax, I love you so much!"

They made love slowly and tenderly, but because they were ignorant of pregnancy and because they had no one to advise them, their lovemaking was cautious, but no less satisfying.

"I think it would be all right to...you know," Carrie whispered later as they lay in each other's arms, too lazy and too content to think of dinner, too wrapped up in each other.

"I don't think we should take any chances," Dax said, then laughed at how prim and stern he sounded.

He kissed her eyelids and the faint smile on her lips, kissed her mounded belly and swollen breasts.

"This is nice," she murmured, stretching. "But I'm worried about you. Abstinence is asking a lot of a man who—"

He silenced her with a kiss, then grinned. "If I recall the last few minutes, we aren't talking about total abstinence. As usual we've found a solution."

She gazed up at him, happiness sparkling in her eyes. "There's no problem that you and I can't solve." They looked at each other and smiled, but the smiles slowly faded. Because there *was* a problem they couldn't solve.

Carrie dropped her head with a frown. She plucked at the folds of the sheet. "Dax, are you going to think about Michael every time you look at the baby?" Her voice was so low that he had to bend his head to hear her.

Laying back on the pillows, he crossed his arms beneath his head and stared at the ceiling. "I wish I could promise you that I won't resent your baby," he said finally. "I wish I could tell you that I'll accept the baby wholeheartedly and love it. But I can't do that, Carrie." He turned his head on the pillow to look at her. "I'm sorry. This is your baby. It will never be mine."

"I'm sorry, too," she whispered, tears thick in her voice. "You'll never know how much I wish this were our baby."

"The best I can do is promise that I'll try very hard not to let the child know I feel no attachment for him or her. But you'll have to love it twice as hard. Because I can't."

She nodded and closed her eyes. He knew she was disappointed, but he couldn't help how he felt.

Long after Carrie had fallen asleep, Dax lay in the darkness struggling with the feeling that he had let her down.

There was nothing he could do about resenting a child that wasn't his. But the problem of being marooned—that was his fault. And it was up to him to find a way out of the mess.

To HELP DEAL with the anxiety of their situation, Carrie returned to her path-building project. Dax swallowed his protests. He recognized that she needed a project to occupy her mind and she needed exercise.

"Just don't overdo," he insisted with a frown, watching her smooth sand inside the rock outline she had arranged.

She was on her hands and knees, her fanny waving in the air. Her delectable bottom hadn't changed one iota. In fact, she was as sexy and desirable as she had always been. It embarrassed him to discover that Carrie's pregnancy hadn't diminished his desire for her. She was radiant and glowing, vibrant and womanly. He responded by wanting her all the time, wanting to caress her and stroke her and cup his hands over the mysterious swell of her belly.

"Quit when you begin to feel tired."

"Stop fussing over me," she said for the hundredth time, smiling at him over her shoulder. "I feel fine. Honest."

He glared at the shrubs lining the path. "Oleander is poisonous, you know."

She rolled her eyes. "I'm not going to eat it or burn it. I'm only smelling the blossoms." A mock frown brought her eyebrows together. "Listen, don't you have some writing to do? I expect to have ten pages to read tonight."

Due in large part to Carrie's insightful suggestions, Dax knew he was producing the best book he had ever written. He was plugging into emotions on a deeper level than he'd previously been capable of doing. As a consequence, his characters were so real that Carrie teased she half expected to look up and see the queen of the vampires leering in the window. Her praise pleased him to an absurd degree. Sometimes he wondered how he had ever produced salable material without her encouragement and suggestions.

"You know I can't write unless you're banging around the house, interrupting me every five minutes," he said, only half joking.

She laughed, flirting with him above her sunglasses. "I'll be there in about an hour. But I warn you, I'm planning a nap. Will snoring be enough of a distraction?"

He grinned, loving her. "Exactly the kind of distraction I need to write at top form."

"Better get started, then. I can't wait to read the next scene."

He gave her a snappy salute but didn't depart immediately. Instead, he stepped back and watched her work on the path, wanting to grab her in his arms and hold her tightly and pour out his heart. He wanted to tell her what she meant to him and how she had changed his thinking and his life.

Because he didn't want her to suspect what he was about to do, Dax made himself leave without sweeping her into his arms and kissing her. She was intuitive and attuned to him. She would have sensed something was going on the minute he touched her.

Quickly he returned to the house and printed out the letter he had written earlier in the day, placing it on Carrie's pillow. Then he retrieved a basket of food and simple medical supplies he had hidden in a nest of ferns beside the foundation. Next he checked the lids on a half dozen bottles of fresh spring water.

When he was certain he hadn't forgotten anything, he changed into jeans and a long-sleeved shirt, jammed a wide-brimmed hat on his head, pushed his sunglasses on his nose, then carried his supplies down to the beach and tied them inside the rubber boat.

After a last glance toward the house, he dragged the boat down the sand and pushed it into the water. When the sea rolled up around his thighs, he climbed into the boat and disengaged the pair of oars.

For a long moment, he sat still, rocking on the waves and studying the watery horizon, reviewing everything he had read about navigation at sea. Without a compass or any other equipment, most of what he had learned was useless. That's why he had chosen to depart in late afternoon. He'd have a chance to orient himself, get the hang of what he was facing while it was still light. When darkness fell, he would use the stars to fix his bearings. He hoped there would be no rain clouds tonight.

He stared at the ocean beyond the sheltering arms of the cove, thinking how intimidating it appeared. On a map twenty-five miles of water looked like a tiny patch. From where Dax sat, the distance seemed enormous, like setting out on an ill-equipped journey for another planet.

It occurred to him there was a negative side to love. Once he would have thrived on a challenge like this, would have welcomed the risk and physical test. Now he felt an uncharacteristic stab of anxiety. He had so much to live for. He had a future he didn't want to risk.

He had Carrie.

Leaning forward, grinding his teeth, he thought about Carrie and the prenatal care she needed, stiffening his resolve, then he dug the oars into the water. Elesia lay due northeast. He would find the island and help—or die trying.

CARRIE'S HEART STOPPED when she found and read the note.

"No!"

Frightened and frantic, she ran down the path to the beach, not stopping until she reached the waterline. "Dax!"

But haze obscured the horizon. There was no sign of him.

Dropping to her knees in the surf, she fought to breathe against the panic that squeezed off her throat. Forgetting her situation, she thought only about him. He didn't know anything about navigation. A violent wave could swamp the boat. A shark might...

"Oh, God!" Burying her face in her hands, she wept until her throat burned and no more tears would come.

Then she dragged herself to the house, the silent, empty house, to pace and worry and wait.

IT WAS a tremendous relief when the sun sank, taking away the searing heat and the blinding reflection bouncing off the water. Dax had tried to use his fresh water sparingly, but it alarmed him to realize how much he drank to replace the sweat pouring off him. Nearly half his supply was gone.

After dipping a towel into the sea, he mopped his face and throat, then stared at the stars overhead, trying to fix his bearings.

He didn't have a clue as to where he was. For all he knew, he'd been traveling in circles for hours. Swearing, he ate one of the Spam sandwiches he had prepared and struggled to calm his thoughts, letting the rubber boat drift with the wash of the waves.

For several minutes he cursed himself for never having taken up sailing. But that was a dead end. Wishing wasn't going to give him the knowledge he needed. Apparently neither was the information he had studied in the encyclopedia. There had been a plentitude of information about navigation, but almost all had addressed the use of equipment Dax did not have. There had been precious little about navigating by the stars.

He rested a minute, letting his mind go blank. His shoulders ached from rowing against the currents. His spine felt like it was breaking. The backs of his neck and hands were fiery red with sunburn. Even his eyes felt scorched and reddened.

He was reaching for the oars again when a tearing, ripping sound sliced through his concentration. Jerking his head up, Dax stared in disbelief at a jagged tip of coral that thrust through the bottom of the boat.

He'd struck a reef. Hissing filled his ears as the rubber boat swiftly deflated around him.

Too shocked to be frightened, he grabbed a life vest and managed to secure the snaps just as the boat melted away beneath him and dropped him into the night-dark sea.

It only took a moment to realize his situation was perilous. He was alone in the middle of the ocean with no expectation of rescue.

He bit down on his back teeth, quelling a flash of panic. He tried to think it through rationally.

He'd been rowing against the current, not making much speed. He couldn't be all that far from the island.

His best hope was to float on the waves and pray that the currents that had brought Carrie to him would carry him back to her.

He bobbed on the water, staring at the distant stars.

"Please, God, take me back to her. Don't leave her alone and helpless. She doesn't deserve that. Please give me another chance to do right by her."

If he made it back to her, he'd never leave her again.

Chapter Thirteen

At dawn, Carrie went down to the beach and sat beside the red-painted SOS rocks, staring at the water until her eyes burned and teared. She didn't really expect to see anything, but she couldn't stay in the silent house. Occasionally, she smoothed out the letter wadded in her hand and reread it. His justifications for leaving her behind made her furious.

Far out beyond the entrance to the cove, she thought she saw a speck of yellow rising and falling with the motion of the waves, but the light wasn't strong enough yet to be sure.

Standing, she ran to the edge of the water, blinking and wiping her eyes, trying to identify the yellow square.

A life vest!

"Dax!" She ran up and down the beach, waving her arms and shouting. As the sun climbed higher, she could see a figure attached to the yellow vest. He was swimming with the currents, his strokes slow and exhausted.

Carrie ran into the water when he entered the cove, wringing her hands and brushing wildly at tears of relief and anger. When he reached her, his face was gray with fatigue. She helped him to the shore and watched him fall in a shaking heap.

"Thank you, God," he whispered, letting his head fall forward on his upraised knees.

"Oh, Dax. Oh, my God." Carrie helped him out of the life vest and flung it behind her. "Are you all right? What happened? Oh, God." She tried to smooth his hair, her hands flying over him. Her emotions tossed together in a crazy mix of numbing relief and furious anger. "How could you do this!"

He pushed back his dripping hair and wiped his hands over his face. "I promised to get you and the baby off this island. I had to try."

"I've never hit anyone in my life, but right now I'd like to punch you out!" She watched his shoulder muscles twitch beneath the shirt plastered to his body. The defeat pinching his mouth and cheeks wrenched her heart. "Are you all right? Tell me you aren't hurt!"

"I'm not hurt. But I failed," Dax said in an exhausted voice. He nodded toward the painted rocks. "What if no one sees our signal? What if no one comes before you go into labor?"

"Do you think that matters? Dax, you could have died out there!"

Sinking to her knees beside him, Carrie burst into tears. She wanted to pummel and hit him, wanted to hold him and love him. The conflicting emotions shook her small frame.

"I'm so mad at you right now," she said when he reached for her. She buried her face in the crease at his neck. His wet clothing soaked her shirt and shorts. "If

I wasn't so grateful that you're alive and unhurt, I'd never speak to you again!"

"I'm sorry, Carrie." His shaking arms went around her and held her tightly.

She looked at him, her eyes flashing angry sparks. "My heart stopped when I read your letter. All I could think about were awful things! Like something terrible happening to you out there. Like you just disappearing and me never knowing what happened." She gripped his wet shoulders and gave him a hard shake. "I kept thinking that something could happen to you and we'd never be married. After I read your letter and discovered what you'd done, I started wondering if marrying you was a good idea, anyway." Her chin lifted and her green eyes locked on his. "Either we're committed to being a team, or we're not. Right now it doesn't look to me like this is much of a partnership. We agreed you wouldn't do this!"

"I thought I was doing the right thing, Carrie, following up the best hope we had to get off this island."

"And look what happened to you!" she snapped. "What happened out there, anyway?"

He told her, his voice slow and furred with fatigue.

Carrie covered her face with her hands as long shudders ran through her body. "Oh, my God! If the currents hadn't flowed toward the island..."

He pulled her into his arms and held her while she cried. "I'm sorry. I didn't know what else to do. I had to try it."

Eventually she quieted, then stood and extended her hand to help him to his feet. "Come on. You need something to eat and some rest."

At the house, Carrie frowned and shooed Norman off the deck, then went into the bathroom and emerged with a couple of towels. "Strip," she ordered, draping his clothing over the deck railing as he peeled it off. "Why didn't the boat hit the reef when I washed into the cove?"

"I don't know," Dax admitted, closing his eyes as she toweled his back and buttocks. "Maybe you came in at high tide and floated over the coral. Or maybe you just missed it." The sun warmed his shaking body. "The boat is gone."

"Good," Carrie said grimly. "You won't be tempted to try this crazy stunt again."

Stepping back, she looked at him standing naked on the deck, ashen with fatigue, his body aglow in the golden rays of the rising sun. His buttocks gleamed pale ivory next to his deeply tanned torso and legs. With his dark hair loose and drying on his shoulders, with his magnificent muscled body, he reminded Carrie of Tarzan. There was an unconscious innocence in his nakedness, an elemental comfort with his natural state.

Abruptly the anger drained out of her, leaving her soft with love for him. Stepping forward, she wrapped her arms around his waist and rested her head against the damp curls on his chest.

"You know," she said softly, "it's going to be hard to go back to civilization and neighbors." Carrie suspected that when she was ninety, she'd be able to close her eyes and see him as he was now, splendidly naked, in the prime of virile manhood, exhausted by his efforts to save and protect her.

He held her tightly, his lips against her hair. "I really am sorry that I worried you. I thought it was the only way."

"I know," she said softly. She had never doubted his motives. Loving had tapped a strong protective urge in Dax. The change amused her, frustrated her, and on this occasion had terrified her. It also made her feel cherished and loved and safe.

"Carrie?" Dax lifted her face and gazed at her with dying eyes. "There's nothing I can do. I can't get us off this damned island. We're stuck here until fate or happenstance rescues us."

"It's all right," she whispered. "We're together."

"Eventually someone will find us. We *will* be rescued." His hands trembled on her cheeks. "I'll spend the rest of our lives making this up to you. I swear it!"

"You don't have— Dax!" Stepping away from him, Carrie looked down, then cupped her stomach with her hands.

"What?"

"Quick! Give me your hand." She pressed his palm against her stomach and watched him as she waited for the baby to move again.

Dax returned her stare with a faintly puzzled expression. "What are we—"

Then the baby stirred and Dax's face shattered in astonishment. While Carrie rubbed at the thrill of goose bumps appearing on her arms, Dax dropped to his knees and pressed his cheek against her stomach.

Suddenly he drew back in surprise, then laughed out loud. "The little dickens kicked me!" he said, lifting a big hand to his face. He gazed up at her. "Oh, my

God," he whispered. Awe shook his voice. "Carrie...you're pregnant! You're going to have a baby!"

Tears choked her laughter. "And I suspect I'm going to have it right here on this island."

Dax sprang to his feet and took her by the elbow, guiding her inside. "Maybe you better sit down. Can I bring you something? A glass of water? A vitamin pill?" Carrie noticed that he had a hand against his own stomach, and she laughed. "Here, let me plump this cushion for your back. Easy now, don't sit down too fast."

Laughing and protesting, she tried to wave him away, but he insisted on fussing over her.

"You're the one who's had a harrowing experience, not me."

But he seemed energized. In a flash she was settled on the sofa, her legs elevated, surrounded by a choice of drinks, vitamins, old magazines and a large chunk of thawed carrot cake.

Dax gazed at her anxiously, wringing his hands. "Is there anything else you need?"

"It would be nice if you put on some clothes." She gave him a roguish look. "I'm having decidedly unmaternal thoughts."

He gave her a shocked stare as he rushed toward the closet.

Carrie shifted on the sofa to watch as he hastily pulled on a pair of fresh cutoffs. "Now don't go strange on me, Dax Stone. Just because I'm pregnant doesn't mean I'll never have another sexy thought."

"But it's *real* now," he said, returning to stare at her stomach. The color had returned to his cheeks. "There's a baby in there."

She lifted her arms and held him close when he knelt beside her. "I have a theory about children. Want to hear it?"

"Tell me."

"Children aren't a gift," she said softly, "they're a loan. We get to have them with us for all too short a time." Easing back, she gazed into his steady eyes. "Someday this child is going to grow up and leave me behind. When that happens, Dax, I want something left between you and me. This baby will be a large part of my life, but I don't want it to be the entire and sole focus. That's too much responsibility for Who's-it, and it wouldn't be good for me, either. When Who's-it goes out into the world, I don't want us to have lost sight of each other."

He touched her cheek. "How did you get to be so smart?" he asked in a gruff voice.

"What I'm saying is, don't make a Madonna out of me, don't treat me differently because I'm going to be a mother. I'm still me. I don't have a halo around my head. All that's changed is that I'm adding another color, a bright, wonderful color, to our personal rainbow."

"You're a pushy little thing," he said, grinning at her. "Always have to have it your way."

"Don't I wish," she said, smiling.

If Carrie could have had things her way, the supply plane would have arrived weeks ago. And she wouldn't be trying so hard not to let Dax guess how frantic she felt about the possibility of coming to term before they were rescued.

THEY BOTH READ everything in the encyclopedia about pregnancy and the birth process. Dax was shaken by the descriptions of all that could go wrong. Several times a day he found his concentration drifting, trying to plan ahead for what he would do if this happened or if that went awry. It was sobering to recognize how helpless they were on the island. Chances were excellent that Carrie would have a normal delivery. But he couldn't help fussing over her and worrying.

"Yes, I took my vitamins. Yes, I had a nice long nap today. Yes, I'm feeling fine," she said, throwing out her hands in exasperation. She looked up from the casserole she was preparing in the kitchen. "Were you always such a worrier?"

"This is different," he said stiffly. Loving her had brought changes he hadn't anticipated. He suspected that the rest of his life would be pricked with worry about things that had previously gone unnoticed. "I don't understand how you can be so calm."

Carrie paused before tucking the casserole into the oven. Now that he had called attention to it, her calmness surprised her a little, too.

During the past two months, a sense of serenity had stolen over her. She no longer felt frantic, and very few things upset her anymore. She was glad she had finished constructing the path to the grotto because she could no longer summon much energy for projects. She was too bulky, in any case.

Recently, when she wasn't going to the bathroom, which she seemed to do constantly, all she wanted was to swing gently in the hammock, think about baby names and surrender to a dreamy state of mind in which her thoughts leapt ahead to the future.

She didn't think about possible problems during delivery, didn't worry about Dax's attitude toward the baby. She didn't want to focus on negatives. In her mind she leapt beyond the delivery. At some point she had accepted that her baby would be born on the island, and she no longer fought the idea. It seemed right somehow.

"What?" Blinking, she opened her eyes and found Dax standing beside her in the kitchen, snapping his fingers under her nose.

"Earth to Carrie... come in, Carrie James."

Smiling, she turned and gave him an awkward hug. Her stomach got in the way of a real embrace. "I'm sorry, I was daydreaming. What did you say?"

"Nothing important," he answered, rolling his dark eyes. "I just asked you to marry me."

Smiling, she touched her fingertips to his lips. "I must be getting senile. I thought we'd already had this conversation. Didn't I say yes?"

Dax took her hand. "I want to marry you before the baby comes. While it's still just you and me. I thought we could write our own vows. Maybe have a ceremony..."

"Why, Dax Stone, you're blushing," Carrie said softly. Her heart swelled with love for him. "For a man who consorts with vampires and ghosts, you're pretty romantic. And I love it!"

"You don't think exchanging vows is... silly, do you?"

Her eyes softened. Reaching for him, Carrie pulled his head down for a long kiss.

"I think marrying ourselves is a lovely, romantic idea."

Tenderly he brushed a tendril of silky chestnut hair off her cheek. "Good. We'll get married tomorrow, then. The minute we're rescued, we'll have a legal ceremony."

Carrie pressed a hand on both sides of his face. "In my mind, tomorrow will always be our real wedding day." A single happy tear leaked from beneath her lashes. "Thank you, Dax."

His warm lips moved over her eyelids. "I love you. You've changed my life, Carrie. You are my life."

They sat together holding hands, watching the sky shade toward pink and lavender. Dax Stone was as happy as he had ever been in his life. The only thing that could have made the moment better was if Carrie's baby could have been his, too. That, and rescue, would have made his life perfect.

CARRIE SURPRISED HERSELF by being more nervous than she had expected to be. She wrote and rewrote her vows a half dozen times, went through her limited wardrobe over and over as if a wedding dress fashioned to accommodate a woman in her eighth month of pregnancy might magically appear if she looked hard enough.

In the end, she decided to wear one of Dax's white long-tailed shirts over an ankle-length sarong-type skirt she fashioned from an extra bed sheet. Her hair was shoulder length now, and she brushed it until it gleamed, then placed a circlet of tropical blossoms on her crown. She carried a bouquet of fragrant thunbergia and delicate ferns.

At the last minute she decided against sandals and walked barefoot to the beach as the sun was starting to set. To her surprise, her fingers were trembling and butterflies fluttered in her stomach.

This was not the wedding she had fantasized about for so many years, the formal gown and packed church. Yet, when she stepped onto the beach and saw Dax standing by the water, waiting for her, her heart soared. And she knew this was the perfect wedding for them. It suddenly seemed strange that she had ever imagined she needed a hundred people to witness an intensely private ceremony. Or that she needed any music beyond the pounding of her heart.

Dax's face lit when he saw her, and he extended his arms. He, too, wore a circlet of blossoms on his head. The collar of a white shirt was open to his waist, and he wore a pair of faded jeans. Like Carrie, he stood barefoot in the sand.

She walked toward the water rolling up the beach, trying not to waddle, trying not to think about being a very pregnant bride.

She was marrying the man she loved more than life itself. Who's-it would have a name and a father. These items were all that mattered. To hell with convention, she thought with a smile. This was her wedding day, the day she had dreamed of all her life.

Dax took both her hands in his, careful not to crush her bouquet, and gazed into her radiant eyes.

"You are so beautiful that you take my breath away!"

Carrie smiled into his eyes, feeling her lashes grow wet with tears of gratitude and happiness. Dax Stone was moody, grouchy on occasion, and she suspected a subtle war of dominance would stimulate their life together. He was also sexy and exciting, generous and caring, loving and tender. She loved him without reserve, with all her pounding heart.

"Before we do this," she whispered, "I want you to be very, very sure, Dax. We've agreed this ceremony is binding on us both. I don't want you to regret it. You're sure, aren't you?"

His eyebrows lifted against his bronzed face. "I won't regret marrying you. I know that." He squeezed her hands. "Carrie, there isn't a doubt in my mind."

She bit her lip, making herself hold his gaze. "I'm talking about the baby," she said in a barely audible voice.

His hesitation told her that nothing had changed. The baby would always be hers. Not theirs. She had to accept that Dax would never feel a connection to the child growing beneath her heart, that his longing for a child of his own would always get in the way.

"This is a package deal," he said, smiling at her. "A two-for-one offer."

It wasn't the answer Carrie yearned to hear. Actually he'd evaded the question. But she had to accept him as he was or not at all.

"Are you ready?" he asked tenderly, pressing her hands and smiling as the breeze off the water ruffled her hair and molded the white shirt against her breasts and swollen stomach.

"Yes." Carrie looked at him with soft eyes that glowed with love for him. She didn't have a doubt in the world. She loved this man with all her heart and soul. She would be loving him fifty years from now, when she drew her last breath.

He stepped close to her, holding her hands and gazing into her upturned face.

"I love you," he said, speaking quietly but firmly. "I promise to cherish you, Carrie, and honor and respect your individuality, your opinions and your desires. From this day forward, you and I are two halves of one whole. I will make no major decision without your full agreement. I promise to abide by compromise if we cannot agree. I vow to love and protect you for the rest of our lives, to seek your happiness as I would seek my own. I will never stand in the way of your personal growth. I will support your endeavors and your goals and make them as important to me as they are to you. I give you everything I own or will ever possess, including my heart and spirit. With these words I marry myself to you now and always."

Tears ran down Carrie's glowing cheeks. Gulls circled above them. Bubbling surf ran up the beach near their bare feet. She was aware of nothing but the love shining in Dax's eyes. She resonated to the harmony of two hearts beating as one, two spirits affirming the joy of finding each other and a future neither had dared hope to find.

"I vow to be your friend, your lover and your wife, to support you fully in all that you do. I promise to be there for you whenever you need me, to share equally in whatever demands life may ask of us. I promise that you will never again be alone."

When she saw the moisture in his eyes, she lifted a trembling hand to his cheek.

"I vow to respect you and your work, to offer help if you ask it, to withdraw if you do not. I promise to love you and care for you in sickness and in health, for richer or for poorer. I will never withhold myself from you but will try with all my heart to be worthy of your love and respect. With these words I wed myself to you now and always.''

"With this ring, I thee wed."

Carrie wiped the tears from her eyes and blinked at the ring he slid onto her finger. She laughed out loud when she saw that he had made a ring out of a Spam strip, binding the metal with green-colored yarn.

Bringing her fingertips to his lips, he turned her hand and kissed her palm. "When we return to Manhattan, I'm going to take you to Tiffany's and buy you the biggest, most expensive, most vulgar diamond in the whole damned place!''

She laughed, the tears beginning again, her heart so full that she wondered if she could contain her happiness. "Where did you get the green yarn?''

"I unraveled a sweater," he said, grinning. "Do I get to kiss the bride?''

"Oh, yes," she said softly, wrapping her arms around his neck.

"My wife," he whispered. His kiss was gentle, reverent, slightly amazed. "My wife!''

Picking her up, he swung her in a circle, his head back, a shout of triumph on his lips. "Hey, world, we're married! This fabulous woman is *mine!*''

"And this splendid man is *mine!*" Carrie shouted, laughing as she collapsed against him. "And I'm never going to let you go!''

"I hope not," Dax said, burying his face against the blossoms in her hair. "I've waited so long for you, Carrie. I've been so lonely and wouldn't admit it. I couldn't bear to lose you now that I've finally found you."

She kissed him hard, then took his hand, her eyes shining. "I used the last of the egg substitute to make us a wedding cake. There's Château Brieoux for you and the last bottle of apple juice for me. Our wedding reception awaits."

Smiling, his chest puffed with pride, Dax offered his arm and escorted her to the house. While Carrie cut the cake, he lit candles around the room and put a tape of romantic classics into the cassette player. This was the happiest day of his life.

"Oh!"

When he looked up, Carrie was standing in the middle of the kitchen, looking down in dismay. Bright crimson embarrassment colored her throat and cheeks.

Frowning, Dax stood. "Carrie? What's wrong?"

"I... This is crazy."

"What?" Her hushed tone brought him around the kitchen counter on the run. He stopped abruptly and blinked at the water gushing down her legs, puddling around her bare feet.

She looked at him apologetically. "I know what this looks like," she said, trying to smile. "But it isn't. I think my water's broken." She spread her hands. "I'm making a hell of a mess, and there's nothing I can do to stop it!"

"Don't worry about the mess," Dax said gruffly. "It's just salt water." Sweeping her into his arms, their hearts hammering in tandem, he carried her into the bathroom and stood her in the glassed-in shower stall. "Give me your clothes and I'll put them in the washer." Her face was pale, looking to him for direction. "When—it—finishes, take a shower, then we'll..." He waved a hand. "I'll boot up the computer and check the encyclopedia."

Mind racing, Dax flung her wet clothing in the washing machine, then cleaned up the puddle in the kitchen. That finished, he hurried to the bathroom, toweled her off and brought her a fresh shirt before he carried her to the bed.

"Are you in pain? Have you had a contraction?"

Her eyes were wide and a deeper shade of green than he had seen them. "I felt something about five minutes ago, but I don't know if it was a contraction. I don't know what a contraction is supposed to feel like." She let him pile pillows behind her back. "Dax..." She bit her lip and looked at her shaking hands. "It's too soon. This shouldn't be happening yet. And I don't think the water is supposed to break before the contractions begin. A dry birth... Well, that isn't good. Is it?"

"Shh." He placed a trembling fingertip across her lips. Reached deep inside for a reassuring smile. "A dry birth occurs when the water breaks and a long time passes before the baby comes. That isn't going to happen. I suspect you're about to have a baby, Mrs. Stone."

Carrie looked at him. He hadn't said *we,* he had said *you.* She wanted the impossible so much. She wanted the illusion that this was their baby.

"Now. You just lay here and try to relax." After sliding his wristwatch off, he handed it to her. "Start timing the length between contractions. Should be about fifteen to twenty minutes between pains," he added briskly.

Carrie managed a small smile. "Been studying the encyclopedia, Dr. Stone?"

Dax smoothed her shower-damp hair off her forehead and sat on the bed beside her, taking her hand. "We're going to get through this, darling. People have been having babies for centuries, long before there were encyclopedias. What the book doesn't tell us, we'll figure out."

She squeezed his hand and rested against the mounded pillows. "I'm glad you're with me. When we're together, I feel there isn't anything we can't do. As long as we're together."

"I wouldn't have missed this for the world."

"Thank you." She didn't know if she believed him, but she loved him for saying it. She squeezed his hand and looked at him with wide, worried eyes. "Maybe it isn't coming early," she said after a minute. "Maybe I miscalculated."

"If the baby's early, it isn't early by much," Dax said, trying to sound confident, like he knew what he was talking about. He patted her hand and made the corners of his mouth turn up. "Can I get you anything? A piece of wedding cake? An aspirin? Some water?" A frown snapped his brows together. *Think,* he commanded himself. *Remember what you read.* "No, nothing to eat or drink. But the aspirin...and shaved ice! Stay here, I'll run some ice cubes through the blender."

"I'm sorry this happened now," Carrie called after him, her hands on her stomach. "On our wedding day."

"What better time? Now we'll have two events to celebrate on this date." Boiling water. He needed boiling water, although he couldn't think why he did. But every description of a delivery included boiling water. Probably for sterilization. He'd sterilize every damned thing he could think of. After slamming around in the cabinets, Dax located their largest pot, filled it to the brim and put the water on the stove to heat.

What next? He slid onto his desk chair and scanned through the encyclopedia pages he pulled up on the screen. "Damn it! They should have given us more information about what exactly a person is supposed to do!" He called to Carrie over his shoulder, "Do you know anything about dilation? How to measure?"

"Not a thing," she said in a small voice that spiraled upward on the last word. When Dax whirled to stare at her, she had both hands pressed against her stomach. "That was definitely a contraction," she said, looking up with a thin smile.

"How long since the first one?" Dax asked, going to her and kneeling beside the bed. Her stomach seemed enormous. A light sheen of perspiration had appeared on her brow.

"About fifteen minutes, I think. Just like you predicted."

"Good. Excellent." He took her hand. "Everything is fine. We're moving right along."

She astonished him by laughing. "Two contractions is not moving right along."

"Okay, we've got a good start. How's that?"

"Better." Shifting uncomfortably, she slipped a hand behind her back.

"Lower back pains?" he inquired anxiously, peering into her face. "That's a good sign. You can stop worrying about a dry birth. Back pain and contractions...it's baby time, love. In a couple of hours you're going to have a perfect healthy baby."

"I hope so," she whispered, staring at the wristwatch as if wishing would hurry things along. "I'm beginning to see why they call this labor. There's a lot of work involved."

"There's nothing to worry about," he assured her. "We're going to sail right through this."

But they didn't sail through it.

Carrie's contractions escalated swiftly into hard, painful jolts that followed swiftly one upon another. Dax was appalled by the pain involved and the effort required. By midnight, she was white and limp with fatigue, and still the baby didn't come.

"I'm so tired," she whispered when Dax lifted her head to give her some shaved ice. "I wish the baby would come."

"I know," he murmured, desperately trying not to sound as anxious and worried as he felt. A sense of frustration and helplessness was eating him alive. "The baby will come soon. He's trying."

Her labor was hard, painful and unrelenting. But the baby didn't come.

At two o'clock, Dax went into the bathroom to wash his face, returning with a cool washcloth for Carrie. He bathed the perspiration off her ashen face, then brought her a fresh shirt to replace the one she had soaked with sweat. When she moved on her side to let him help her with the shirt, he froze, noticing a trickle of watery blood that stained the sheets beneath her exhausted body. His heart slammed behind his rib cage. His breath stopped in his chest.

Rigid with shock and worry, he stared at her pale, tired face, at the fine lines of pain deepening beside her mouth and closed eyes. Her body was damp with perspiration, instantly soaking the clean shirt. Groaning, she bent forward as another contraction wracked her body.

And still the baby didn't come.

At three, Dax sank to the floor beside the bed, clasping her hand against his heart, murmuring her name through a tight throat. Her pulse was weak and thready, terrifying him. More blood seeped onto the sheet.

"I love you, Carrie," he said. His chest was tight and he felt hollow, as if fear had scooped out his insides. He couldn't stop shaking. Lowering his head to the edge of the bed, he closed his eyes and ground his teeth together.

"Something's wrong," she whispered, gripping his hand weakly. "I...don't think I'm going to make it."

"Don't say that!"

But the same fear had occurred to him. She was bleeding and dangerously weak, suffering so much. He would have given anything if he could have taken her pain on himself and spared her.

Dax hadn't prayed in years, but he did so now.

Chapter Fourteen

At four in the morning the contractions inexplicably ceased. Almost instantly Carrie lapsed into an exhausted sleep, her breathing shallow and ragged with pain. When Dax called her name, she didn't stir.

Frantic, he stood and paced in front of the bed, walking off the cramps gripping his leg muscles. Gradually he became aware of an acrid burning smell and hurried into the kitchen. Long ago the water had boiled out of the pot on the stove. Scorched metal glistened on the burner.

After turning off the burner, he flattened his palms on the countertop and let his head drop between his shoulders. Tears of helplessness and fear clogged his throat. Rage shook his big body.

How could God, fate, the powers that be—whoever or whatever—do this to Carrie and to him? It was not fair! For the first time in his life he had someone of his own. He was no longer lonely or alone. Because of Carrie he was discovering a new and better world. And Carrie... Carrie was sweet and kind and understanding and good. She was a shining flame of honesty and generosity, the one thing that made his life worth living.

And she was dying.

Carrie, who was so quick to smile, so eager to offer a helping hand or a word of optimism and encouragement, so forgiving and open and alive. The world would be a cold, icy rock without Carrie James Stone. Dax rejected such a world. He didn't want to be part of a universe that could let Carrie die.

He raised his hands and rubbed burning eyes. God. He had to *do* something. Anything. What? Was there anything he *could* do? Even if it was hopeless, futile, he had to do something to help her or go insane.

After checking to see that she was still sleeping, her chest hardly rising, he breathed deeply against his panic, then grabbed the wicker chairs and ran them down to the beach, an idea growing in his desperate mind. Next he dragged the sofa to the beach and piled cushions on it. He added the coffee table and the end tables to the pile he was building.

Carrie slept and moaned softly through his frenzied trips back and forth from the house. He couldn't tell if she was asleep or unconscious, and was too terrified to dwell on the possibilities.

He knelt beside her, bathing her face and throat, tears glistening in his eyes. "I love you. I love you. Don't leave me, Carrie. Keep fighting, darling. It's going to be all right. Be strong for us." Bending over her, he smoothed her damp hair and placed a kiss on her lips. "I'll return in a few minutes."

Grabbing up a handful of manuscript pages, he sprinted to the beach and the huge pile of furniture.

Moving swiftly, he wadded pages of his new book and pushed them under chair legs, between cushions. Hands shaking, he ran around the pile, lighting the pages, standing back as the flames caught hold, silently urging the fire to soar and burn bright.

The dry wicker ignited with a soft, explosive whoosh. In minutes a roaring blaze burned red and orange against the black night, lighting the sky.

Dax paced in front of the blaze, his furious scowl directed at the moonless sky. He raised both fists and roared his pain into the night.

"Listen to me, God! Can you see me? Here I am, and I'm talking to you. I'm begging you! Let Carrie live. If there's a shred of mercy and compassion in you, then let her live! If you have to have someone, take me!" He threw back his shaggy head and bellowed in rage and fear and helplessness. "Do you hear me, God? Take me! Carrie never hurt anyone. She didn't do anything wrong! She doesn't deserve to suffer and die, damn it! Take me and *let her live!*"

Dropping to his knees on the fire-shadowed sand, he covered his face in both hands and sobbed as he hadn't done since he was a child.

"I beg you. Don't do this. Don't let us find each other after all these lonely years, then give us only a few short months together. I'm begging you, God. I'll do anything, just please save her. Save her!"

His eyes burned with scalding tears, and his throat was raw from shouting.

Stumbling to his feet and cursing, Dax threw another piece of furniture on the fire, then spun and raced to the house. The first bluish hint of dawn lighted his way.

"Dax!"

He wouldn't have heard her weak whisper if it hadn't been deathly quiet. "I'm here, darling. I'm here." Rushing forward, he clasped her hand.

A hard contraction drew her body tight, and she jerked her hand away. When the contraction passed, she fell back on the pillows, gasping and exhausted, her face gray with pain.

"Breathe," he urged her, smoothing her brow with a shaking hand. "Try to relax." He didn't know what he was saying. Her face was so ashen that her freckles stood out like splatters of paint. She gripped the sheet with weak, bloodless fingers.

"The baby..." she whispered, panting. "Coming...." He didn't know how she could survive any more pain, any more labor. Grinding his teeth, swallowing the tears scalding his throat, Dax leapt to his feet and ran to the kitchen, where he had long ago prepared a parcel of sterilized items. He scrubbed his hands at the sink, running the water as hot as he could bear, glancing outside the window at the futile flames roaring on the beach, flickering through the palms and underbrush.

Hurrying to Carrie, murmuring an encouraging babble of words that he didn't hear, he carefully drew back the sheet covering her straining form, then sucked in a hard, painful breath.

The sheet below her body was bright red with blood.

"Oh, God," he whispered, feeling the strength ebb out of his body. "Oh God, please!"

"The baby... coming," she gasped as another contraction swept her.

There wasn't time to change the sheet. All Dax could do was place the folded sterile sheets on top of the bloody one, easing them between her legs and beneath her body.

The contractions came hard and fast, tumbling one over another, not allowing her time to rest between and regain a little strength.

"Dax... if I don't..."

He kneeled on the bed between her legs, sweating, swallowing convulsively, his heart hammering violently against his chest.

"The baby's coming!" he said, glancing at her white, white face. "Don't give up now, darling. Be strong!"

"Make it, I want you... to know... you were the best thing... that ever happened to me."

"You will make it!" His dark eyes burned on her face, willing his strength into her, loving her so hard that his big body shook with emotion. "Your baby needs you! I need you! Push, Carrie. We're so close, my love!"

"Trying... love you... so much."

A wet red face emerged, then two tiny shoulders. And a gush of blood. So much blood that it shocked Dax and prickled his skin with fear.

"One more push, darling! One more!"

Goose bumps raced up and down his spine. The miracle he witnessed brought tears of intense emotion to his eyes and made him tremble. A turbulent mix of fear and elation churned his mind, turned his knees to pudding.

"Hang on, dearest, my darling love. One more push. You can do it, Carrie, you're the bravest woman I've ever met. We're almost there, love, it's almost over."

A tiny warm bundle slid into his waiting hands. And another gush of blood. He stared at the crimson rush as Carrie fell back against the pillows, too weak to wipe the tears that dripped down the sides of her face.

He needed more time—there wasn't time to do all that had to be done. Swiftly he scooped his finger inside the baby's mouth, checking for obstructions as the encyclopedia had instructed, then he used sterile towels to hastily clean the infant's face and chest. And his heart ceased beating when he noticed the baby was not breathing.

"Breathe!" he shouted, staring hard into the tiny face. "Breathe, damn it, breathe!"

Panic seared his mind before he grabbed control of his thoughts. A thousand film scenes flashed in his brain. Hell, he'd written a scene like this himself.

Lifting the baby by tiny ankles, he slapped its behind and prayed out loud. "Do it! Breathe!" Nothing happened. He gave the infant another slap, cringing as he did so. It was so tiny.

A blessed gasp filled his ears like a symphony followed by an outraged cry. The tiny red chest swelled, sucking in air, and a lusty cry emerged.

Dax closed his eyes. A tremor shook his arms and legs. "Thank you," he whispered. "Thank you, God." Moving rapidly, he tied off the umbilical cord as the encyclopedia had instructed, then wrapped a sterilized bath towel around the child.

"I'd be mad, too," he said softly to the cries of protest, using his thumb to smooth back damp strands of silky hair. "You've had a hell of a first few minutes. Now stay here, don't go away." Carefully, he placed the bundled child at Carrie's side, away from the bright blood, then he sponged the sweat off her face.

Her color had faded to a lifeless white. Her lips were bluish. Deep purplish shadows circled her eyes like bruises.

"Carrie? Carrie, can you hear me?" Rigid with fear, he frantically rubbed her hand, trying to infuse his strength into her weak body. Her shallow breathing terrified him.

"Too...much blood," she whispered. Her eyelids lifted, then closed. "Not going...to make it."

Dax heard the door open behind him and jumped when he heard a man's deep voice.

"Ah, excuse me?"

Whirling, Dax jumped to his feet and feasted his eyes on the most welcome sight he had ever seen. He stared at the man in the doorway and the strength ran out of his body like water. He thought he might collapse. "Thank God!"

"I saw your fire on the beach. Saw the SOS rocks on my way up to the house. You folks need help?"

"God, yes!" Dax stumbled forward, almost fell on the man. Tears glistened in his eyes. "Did you come by boat or helicopter?"

The man wiped his hands over a fishing jacket and peered behind Dax at the bloodied sheets and Carrie's limp form. He swept a crushed hat off a thatch of graying hair. The wrinkles pleating his face deepened in sympathetic concern, then urgency as he took in the situation. "Fishing boat. Motorized. How new is that baby?"

"About ten minutes. Please, I beg you. My wife is dying. She's bleeding profusely. We need a medical team and a helicopter! And for God's sake, watch out for the reef! Please. Go! Get us help!"

"I've fished this cove before, I know about the reef. Give me an hour and a half, two hours tops." The man pressed Dax's arm, glanced at Carrie, then dashed out of the house.

Dax closed his eyes, swaying on his feet. "Thank you, God! But stay on the job, okay? The story doesn't end here. This is our opening chapter, it isn't the final scene."

Whirling, he returned to Carrie. There were things he could do. He packed towels between her legs and sponged off her face, made her swallow some aspirin to fight the fever that burned beneath her clammy gray skin.

Her lashes fluttered and she tried to speak but no audible words emerged. He saw her lips form the word *what*.

"It was a man, an angel. He's gone for help." He clasped her hand against his racing heart. "Hang on, darling, don't give up now. Help will arrive soon!"

Her eyelids fluttered. Dax stared hard at the clean sheet he had drawn up around her. He didn't see it move, didn't see her breathe. Panic scorched his chest.

"Carrie! Breathe!"

Her lids flickered. She seemed confused and far away. Then her eyes found his face and cleared for an instant. She tried to lick her lips. "The baby?"

Oh, God. Of course. Leaning over her, he lifted the warm, small bundle and carefully, tenderly placed the baby on her breast, folding her arms around it.

"We have a daughter," he whispered, "a beautiful daughter." Tears spilled over his lashes as he gazed at them. Never had Dax seen anything as beautiful or as moving as this mother and newborn child.

Shock widened his eyes. He had said *we* have a daughter. He didn't stop to analyze the slip of the tongue. He rubbed Carrie's hand and stared into her face, watching the life ebb away, furious and despairing that he didn't know how to help her, how to save her.

"Happy," she mouthed at him, her eyelids closing. "You?"

"Darling, I've never been happier."

Then he knelt beside the bed, dropped his head in his hands and wept.

He didn't know how much time passed. But eventually he understood he had lost her.

His strength and willpower, his love were not enough to keep Carrie alive.

At the end she opened her eyes and gazed at him. She tried so hard to smile that her effort broke his heart. Her hand stirred in his. "I..." Then a weak shudder ran through her body and her head rolled forward against the baby's hair. She lay still.

A roar of rage and anguish bellowed up from Dax's toes, and he felt a pain so intense that it blinded him. *"No!"*

His screams of protest drowned the noise erupting through the door until a rough arm shoved him aside, almost knocking him off his feet.

"Stand back! Damn it, get out of the way!"

People ran in the door, hauling equipment, shouting, shoving, jerking the bed away from the wall. A man in a white coat leaned over Carrie, shouting and performing CPR. Someone else shoved a needle in her arm. A woman in white took the baby, held it while a man lifted the infant's eyelids and put drops in her eyes. A half dozen people yelled and talked at once.

A large, rough hand clasped Dax's shoulder and turned him toward the door. "Come outside. Let the experts do their job. You're only in the way here." It was the fisherman who had spotted his fire.

At first Dax resisted, then he accepted the truth of the suggestion and, stumbling with hope and exhaustion, he let himself be led down to the beach. His rescuer guided him to a shaded spot in sight of the pile of smoldering embers. Though it was early morning, the sun was already hot, blazing behind a high, thin haze.

"Here." The fisherman removed a pint of whiskey from his vest and extended the bottle to Dax. "Take a slug. Looks like you could use a drink."

Dax swallowed gratefully, feeling a hot jolt explode in his stomach. He wiped a hand across his mouth, saw Carrie's blood on his shirt and took another long pull.

"She's gone. I've lost her." He stared through a film of moisture at the pair of Flight for Life helicopters on the beach without really seeing them. An open door revealed a gurney bolted to the bulkhead and banks of medical monitoring equipment.

"The name's Wes Patterson. Thank God I saw your fire. I haven't fished near this island in months. Glad I came this way this morning. Didn't think this island was inhabited. How long you and your wife been here?"

"It's a long story." Dax took another pull on the bottle, letting the whiskey wash over the ice that had settled in the pit of his stomach. He felt exhausted and sick with grief.

"Look," he said rubbing a hand over the stubble on his jawline. "Wes, is it? Wes, I can't sit here while they're . . . I have to go back. Carrie . . . she—"

He broke off speaking as two men ran down the path and onto the beach. One of them shouted to the helicopter pilots.

"Fire 'em up, we're leaving!" He turned aside and spoke urgently into a hand-held radio, waving one blood-splattered arm.

The rest of the team flew into sight, then, half pushing, half carrying a gurney. Dax saw Carrie's hair above a sheet. Her face was as white as the pillow supporting her head. Two men ran beside her, holding aloft plastic drip bags. Last to emerge was the woman carrying the baby.

"Let's go, people, let's go, let's go! Move!"

Wes Patterson gripped Dax's arm and propelled him toward the second helicopter. They ducked beneath whirling blades, helped the woman with the baby inside, then followed her. The first helicopter carrying Carrie had already lifted into the sky, was banking sharply to the northeast.

The instant they were belted in, Dax turned pleading eyes to the woman. The name badge on her white coat identified her as Norma Watson.

"Is my wife alive?" His heart and soul shook in his voice.

Nurse Watson gazed at him with large brown eyes soft with sympathy. "Just barely. Mr. . . ."

"Stone. Dax Stone." He didn't know if it was the sound of the helicopter or the noise of his heart slamming around inside his chest, but he could hardly hear her.

"Your wife is a fighter, Mr. Stone, and the best people available are awaiting her arrival at the Elesia hospital." She hesitated, then said what he so clearly wanted to hear. "She'll make it."

Norma Watson and Wes Patterson looked aside as Dax dropped his head and wept unashamedly.

Minutes before the helicopter swept out of the skies toward the landing pad atop the hospital, Mrs. Watson stroked a finger across the baby's cheek, then smiled at Dax.

"Your daughter is fine, Mr. Stone. You have a perfect, healthy little girl. What's her name?"

"Caroline," he blurted. "Like her mother."

The helicopter touched down, and Dax leapt out. A team of white coats swarmed around the first copter.

In seconds, Carrie was being wheeled inside. Dax sprinted after her, shoving people aside until he was running down a tiled corridor beside her, holding her hand.

She squeezed his fingers and her eyelids fluttered open. "Dax." The corridor was filled with noise, clattering wheels, people talking and shouting, doors banging open, but he heard only her whisper.

"I'm here, darling, right beside you."

"So tired."

"I know." Ahead of the gurney someone threw open the doors to an operating room. Dax saw a green-suited team waiting inside, masked, gloved hands in the air. "Fight, love. We need you!"

She glanced at the drip bottles above her, the faces, and tried to smile. "Good scene . . . for the book."

Someone grabbed him as the gurney shot through the operating room doors. "You can't go in there. Wait outside, please."

The doors swung shut in his face.

Wes Patterson stepped up beside him. "There's coffee in the cafeteria."

Dax stared at the closed doors, his fists clenched at his sides. "She'll make it!" he said fiercely. "She will!"

Sympathy filled Patterson's eyes, and he looked at the hat he twisted in his hands. "I hope so."

"She's small, but she's pushy as hell. Has to have everything her way. God isn't going to take Carrie before she's damned good and ready to go!"

Wes Patterson smiled. "Come on, son. Let's find your daughter and make sure she's all right, then we'll get some coffee."

Dax stared hard at the closed doors.

Hang in there, Carrie. Fight, darling! Fight for our future, for you and me and our daughter.

Three hours later, Dr. Evencourt came to the cafeteria looking for him.

DAX PUSHED THROUGH the door of Room 425 and paused just inside to look toward the bed. A wave of gratitude and melting relief flooded his body and left him shaky in the knees for a moment. He felt his throat tighten with emotion.

Carrie was sitting up today, humming softly and cradling the baby in her tanned arms. A nurse had placed an emerald ribbon in her hair, and she wore the lacy bed jacket Dax had bought for her. She looked so radiant that he wouldn't have guessed she was still weak from her ordeal if he hadn't seen the drip bottles above her bed, hadn't spoken twice daily to her doctor. The shadows had nearly faded from beneath her eyes. Roses blossomed on her cheeks.

Sensing his presence, Carrie lifted her head, and her face lit at the sight of him. "More flowers?" she asked, smiling. "This room is starting to look like a floral shop." Her eyes glowed. "And I love it."

Dax handed the roses to a nurse and took the chair beside the bed, catching her hand between both of his. "How are you feeling today?"

"Well enough to notice that you got a haircut. You look so handsome I'll bet all the nurses swoon when you walk past."

He laughed. "I doubt it. One of them inquired when the next book was due out, then asked if I really believed in vampires. I think they're scared to death of me." Leaning forward, he kissed her lips. "Seriously, how are you feeling?"

"I'm ready to get out of here."

"Not for at least another week," he said, pressing her hand against the linen jacket he wore. "We're not taking any chances."

God, he loved the look of her. Loved the way her freckles moved toward each other when she smiled, loved the green sparkle in her eyes and the tousled curls framing her cheekbones. He loved how her expression lit when she looked at him, loved the way she made him feel as if he were ten feet tall. He didn't know what he had ever done to deserve this wonderful woman, but he planned to spend the rest of his life striving to be worthy of her.

"I spoke to your parents," he said in a gruff voice. "Did they phone you?"

She nodded, smiling into the baby's sleeping face. "They're catching the next plane to the islands. They can't wait to meet you and Caroline." She raised an eyebrow and narrowed her gaze in a mock frown. "You might have consulted me about the name, by the way. I was considering Tiffany, or maybe Holly."

"No way," he said, grinning. "This is a tough little girl, just like her mother. A pushy little thing. She's a Carrie if I ever saw one."

"Would you like to hold her?"

"Me?" He cast an uncertain look at the bundle cradled against Carrie's breast. Then he swallowed hard and extended his arms, feeling big and clumsy and awkward.

"Did you find out what happened to Mort? And why the supply plane didn't arrive?"

"Hmm?" He gazed down at the tiny face surrounded by the folds of a light pink blanket. "Mort was in a plane crash. He was in a coma until two weeks ago. It's still touch and go. His secretary burst into tears when I phoned. She's been worried half out of her mind, tearing the office apart trying to find some clue as to where I was."

"I love you, Dax," Carrie said softly, resting against the pillows, smiling at him. "I love you with all my heart." She nodded at the baby and spoke in a low voice. "It's going to be all right, isn't it? The baby?"

Caroline startled him by opening her eyes and gazing up at him with a crinkled, solemn expression.

"Hi," he said softly, looking down at her. "Remember me?" He could have sworn she gave him a tiny smile of recognition and snuggled closer to his body. Something totally unexpected happened. A feeling like warm molasses poured through Dax's body and melted his heart. His throat swelled painfully.

"Ah, Caroline," he whispered, holding her protectively against his chest, looking into her face. "I think you've made your first conquest." He stroked one large finger over her tiny cheek. Moisture glistened in his eyes. "I'm afraid I see our future, little Carrie. You're going to twist me around your little finger, aren't you? Just like your beautiful mother."

He had not sired this small bundle that he held in his arms. But he saw now that it didn't matter. Caroline was his baby. He had helped bring her into this world, and he would help her travel through it. And God help the poor bastard who ever hurt her. Dax would tear him limb from limb.

He raised damp eyes to Carrie. "She's ours."

A knock sounded at the door, and Wes Patterson poked his head inside. "May I come in? I brought my wife to meet you folks."

Dax sat on the bed, one arm around Carrie, the other cradling Caroline close to his chest. "Mrs. Patterson, I'd like you to meet my wife, Carrie, and my daughter, Caroline. This is my family." They were the sweetest words he had ever uttered.

Mrs. Patterson smiled at Carrie, then bent to admire the baby snuggling in Dax's arms.

"She's a beautiful child," Mrs. Patterson cooed. "I believe she has your nose and chin, Mr. Stone. The resemblance is unmistakable."

"She does?" Eyes wide, Dax bent to study his daughter's face. "By God, she does!" His chest puffed with pride. A huge smile split his face. "Carrie! Did you notice this, darling? She has my chin and nose! She really does!"

Carrie leaned her head against his broad shoulder and gazed up at him, her eyes shining with tears of love and happiness.

It was going to be all right. Dax and Caroline were falling in love in front of her eyes. She should have known better than to worry.

Dax's stories always had a happy ending.

HARLEQUIN®

A M E R I C A N ◆ R O M A N C E®

You asked for it...you've got it. More MEN!

We're thrilled to bring you another special edition of the popular
MORE THAN MEN series.

Like those who have come before him, Chase Quinn is more than tall,
dark and handsome. All of these men have extraordinary powers that
make them "more than men." But whether they are able to grant you
three wishes or live forever, make no mistake—their greatest, most
extraordinary power is of seduction.

So make a date in October with Chase Quinn in

#554 THE INVISIBLE GROOM
by Barbara Bretton

SUPH6

MILLION DOLLAR SWEEPSTAKES (III)

No purchase necessary. To enter, follow the directions published. Method of entry may vary. For eligibility, entries must be received no later than March 31, 1996. No liability is assumed for printing errors, lost, late or misdirected entries. Odds of winning are determined by the number of eligible entries distributed and received. Prizewinners will be determined no later than June 30, 1996.

Sweepstakes open to residents of the U.S. (except Puerto Rico), Canada, Europe and Taiwan who are 18 years of age or older. All applicable laws and regulations apply. Sweepstakes offer void wherever prohibited by law. Values of all prizes are in U.S. currency. This sweepstakes is presented by Torstar Corp., its subsidiaries and affiliates, in conjunction with book, merchandise and/or product offerings. For a copy of the Official Rules send a self-addressed, stamped envelope (WA residents need not affix return postage) to: MILLION DOLLAR SWEEPSTAKES (III) Rules, P.O. Box 4573, Blair, NE 68009, USA.

EXTRA BONUS PRIZE DRAWING

No purchase necessary. The Extra Bonus Prize will be awarded in a random drawing to be conducted no later than 5/30/96 from among all entries received. To qualify, entries must be received by 3/31/96 and comply with published directions. Drawing open to residents of the U.S. (except Puerto Rico), Canada, Europe and Taiwan who are 18 years of age or older. All applicable laws and regulations apply; offer void wherever prohibited by law. Odds of winning are dependent upon number of eligibile entries received. Prize is valued in U.S. currency. The offer is presented by Torstar Corp., its subsidiaries and affiliates in conjunction with book, merchandise and/or product offering. For a copy of the Official Rules governing this sweepstakes, send a self-addressed, stamped envelope (WA residents need not affix return postage) to: Extra Bonus Prize Drawing Rules, P.O. Box 4590, Blair, NE 68009, USA.

SWP-H794

This summer, come cruising with Harlequin Books!

PORTS
OF CALL

In July, August and September, excitement, danger and, of course, romance can be found in Lynn Leslie's exciting new miniseries PORTS OF CALL. Not only can you cruise the South Pacific, the Caribbean and the Nile, your journey will also take you to Harlequin Superromance®, Harlequin Intrigue® and Harlequin American Romance®.

- ◆ In July, cruise the South Pacific with SINGAPORE FLING, a Harlequin Superromance
- ◆ NIGHT OF THE NILE from Harlequin Intrigue will heat up your August
- ◆ September is the perfect month for CRUISIN' MR. DIAMOND from Harlequin American Romance

So, cruise through the summer with LYNN LESLIE and HARLEQUIN BOOKS!

CRUISE

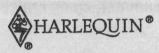

® HARLEQUIN ®

Weddings, Inc.

THE WEDDING GAMBLE
Muriel Jensen

Eternity, Massachusetts, was America's wedding town. Paul Bertrand knew this better than anyone—he never should have gotten soused at his friend's rowdy bachelor party. Next morning when he woke up, he found he'd somehow managed to say "I do"—to the woman he'd once jilted! And Christina Bowman had helped launch so many honeymoons, she knew just what to do on theirs!

THE WEDDING GAMBLE, available in September from American Romance, is the fourth book in Harlequin's new cross-line series, **WEDDINGS, INC.**

Be sure to look for the fifth book, **THE VENGEFUL GROOM,** by Sara Wood (Harlequin Presents #1692), coming in October.

WED4

A NEW STAR COMES OUT TO SHINE....

American Romance continues to search the heavens for the best new talent... the best new stories.

Join us next month when a new star appears in the American Romance constellation:

Kim Hansen
#548 TIME RAMBLER
August 1994

Even in the shade of a broad-rimmed Stetson, Eagle River's lanky sheriff had the bluest eyes Katie Shannon had ever seen. But why was he in the ghost town—a man who was killed in a shoot-out one hundred years ago?

Be sure to Catch a "Rising Star"!

STAR2

This September, discover the fun of falling in love with...

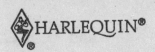

love and laughter

Harlequin is pleased to bring you this exciting new collection of three original short stories by bestselling authors!

ELISE TITLE
BARBARA BRETTON
LASS SMALL

LOVE AND LAUGHTER—sexy, romantic, fun stories guaranteed to tickle your funny bone and fuel your fantasies!

Available in September wherever
Harlequin books are sold.

◆ HARLEQUIN®

Pencil Us In...
1995 Calendars from
the Romance Experts.

Plan ahead with three fabulous new calendars!

REPORTING ON ROMANCE
A 1995 Daily Calendar
$8.99 U.S./$12.99 CAN.

MAVERICK HEARTS*
16 Months of
Heartbreaking Hunks
$12.99 U.S./$15.99 CAN.

WITH LOVE,
FROM HARLEQUIN'S
KITCHEN 1995
Delicious confections for
Gift Giving
$9.95 U.S./$13.99 CAN.

*Plus a FREE Country & Western Cassette
featuring such bestselling recording artists as:
Alan Jackson, Clint Black, Brooks & Dunn
and many more!
A $10 value, absolutely FREE with
the purchase of MAVERICK HEARTS!

Available this fall at your favorite retail outlet.

HARLEQUIN® and Silhouette®

CAL1

HARLEQUIN®

Don't miss these Harlequin favorites by some of our most
distinguished authors!
And now you can receive a discount by ordering two or more titles!

HT #25525	THE PERFECT HUSBAND by Kristine Rolofson	$2.99	☐
HT #25554	LOVERS' SECRETS by Glenda Sanders	$2.99	☐
HP #11577	THE STONE PRINCESS by Robyn Donald	$2.99	☐
HP #11554	SECRET ADMIRER by Susan Napier	$2.99	☐
HR #03277	THE LADY AND THE TOMCAT by Bethany Campbell	$2.99	☐
HR #03283	FOREIGN AFFAIR by Eva Rutland	$2.99	☐
HS #70529	KEEPING CHRISTMAS by Marisa Carroll	$3.39	☐
HS #70578	THE LAST BUCCANEER by Lynn Erickson	$3.50	☐
HI #22256	THRICE FAMILIAR by Caroline Burnes	$2.99	☐
HI #22238	PRESUMED GUILTY by Tess Gerritsen	$2.99	☐
HAR #16496	OH, YOU BEAUTIFUL DOLL by Judith Arnold	$3.50	☐
HAR #16510	WED AGAIN by Elda Minger	$3.50	☐
HH #28719	RACHEL by Lynda Trent	$3.99	☐
HH #28795	PIECES OF SKY by Marianne Willman	$3.99	☐

Harlequin Promotional Titles

#97122	LINGERING SHADOWS by Penny Jordan	$5.99	☐
	(limited quantities available on certain titles)		

	AMOUNT	$
DEDUCT:	10% DISCOUNT FOR 2+ BOOKS	$
	POSTAGE & HANDLING	$
	($1.00 for one book, 50¢ for each additional)	
	APPLICABLE TAXES*	$_____
	TOTAL PAYABLE	$_____
	(check or money order—please do not send cash)	

To order, complete this form and send it, along with a check or money order for the
total above, payable to Harlequin Books, to: **In the U.S.:** 3010 Walden Avenue,
P.O. Box 9047, Buffalo, NY 14269-9047; **In Canada:** P.O. Box 613, Fort Erie, Ontario,
L2A 5X3.

Name: _____

Address:_____City: _____

State/Prov.: _____ Zip/Postal Code: _____

*New York residents remit applicable sales taxes.
 Canadian residents remit applicable GST and provincial taxes..

HBACK-JS